WITH YOUR PERMISSION

In The Heart Of A Valentine Book 5

STEPHANIE NICOLE NORRIS

To the reader who is unsure about love. Never give up. All things happen in due time.

Chapter One

L'ÉCOLE FRANÇAISE, CHICAGO

"*R*emember, you don't have to pout your lips, but it may help if you do. Now, repeat after me. *Puis-je.*"

Bri St. James followed the motion of Raphael's succulent brown lips as he spoke in French on his third attempt to correct her pronunciation.

"*Puis-je,*" she repeated.

"*Avoir des fruits.*"

"*Avoir des fruits.*"

"Excellent," he said, a grin lifting the corners of his delicious mouth. "You've earned a strawberry," his dark voice drummed, easing the saucer of strawberries across the table.

Bri returned his smile, the inside of her body swelling with heat from the sexual chemistry of the language of love.

Today was the first day of her foreign linguistic course, and she was being taught by the one and only Raphael Valentine, world-renowned photographer.

Bri had Allison Sullivan to thank for it. As Bri's best friend of sixteen years, Allison had presented her with the opportunity to coordinate the wedding of Hunter Valentine, CEO of VFC Energy, and a pregnant Camilla Augustina, anchor at WTZB. The two were the hottest Chicago celebrity couple at the time, and Allison had become newly acquainted with Camilla since the two were co-workers at the news station.

Being the founder of Building Bridges Wedding and Event Planning, Bri was ecstatic to take on the project. Meeting the celebrity family was a highlight for her, especially because Raphael's media mogul parents, Leslie and Bridgette Valentine had been behind some of the channels that broadcasted Bri's up and coming achievements. Throughout the years, she remained the humbled enthusiastic go-getter she started as, even as her company won international awards, taking her business to new heights.

While working on said project, Bri came in contact with Hunter's five brothers, each man the most sought after in his career. Raphael Valentine broke through the mold. He'd caught Bri's eye at the wedding rehearsal and slipped into a conversation by happenstance.

Bri was surveying the area like she always did once her décor was in place for the main event. After giving directions and walking past a vase of multi-colored tulips, she heard a deep, authoritative voice speak out.

"Those used to be her favorite."

Bri swirled quickly to her left, coming to face the wide stretch of an extended torso sheathed behind a white button-down shirt. Her eyes ran up his broad shoulders and a thick stake of muscle that was his throat, into heavy piercing eyes, dark with a blue hue that colored the edges of his irises.

Damn.

He was clearly a part of the family since his striking features, rich chocolate skin, and muscle tone resembled that of his brothers. How she missed him thus far was unbeknown to her, but the important thing was now that they had met, she needed to know who the *her* was he'd referred to.

"Forgive me," he apologized. "I couldn't help but notice the tulips. My fiancée brought them home fresh every day with a smile on her face." The sparkle in his eye dimmed. "That was before she passed."

Bri's gasp was soft but surprising nonetheless.

"I...I'm sorry," she said, almost speechless and feeling as if she needed to say more. When Bri couldn't find the words, she instinctively stepped into the cover of his shadow and embraced him with a hug.

Raphael's initial reaction was tense as his body went rigid from her containment, but he thawed immediately, simultaneously questioning the splintering zing that shot through his loins at her soft caress.

Without a lengthy contemplation, his arms curved around her shoulders, and heat enveloped them both in a blanket of warmth.

An audible breath escaped Bri's lips on a hum just as a

mutiny of nerves settled in the base of her belly, colluding with her body without the necessary consent from her. She found herself sinking into him further; the warmth from his solid physique making her spirit hyper and her stomach flip with somersaults. They leaned into one another that day as if they were old friends holding tight to the comfort of their burdens. But the sad moment turned their sorrow into a lustful unencumbered situation, one that was unexpected and tempted their libidos on another level. It became hard for Bri to let him go as the scent of his cologne and manly aura seeped into her nostrils, lulling her to another universe. It was only when Philip, Bri's business partner and photographer, strolled up beside them with a clearing of his throat that she blinked out of her haze.

"Um, excuse me, Brittney?"

"Huh?" Bri's brows arched, and as if regaining consciousness she came out of the trance, slowly untangling herself from Raphael's hold to take a step back.

Even though Philip called her, Bri's eyes were turned up to Raphael's as she wondered if he felt the same desire race through his gut as she.

Philip continued, though he was half-ignored.

"When you get a second, I need you to recheck the area for family photos. I'm not sure about the lighting, but you know I can make it work if I need to."

In his early forties, Philip's tall, lanky build hovered as he blinked between Bri and Raphael, then he scratched the top of his bald coffee-toned head and wondered why Bri was so fascinated with Raphael. Philip sized him up, then rolled his eyes. If it was going to take dragging Bri away to get her focus on him, Philip just might do it.

Finally pulling her gaze away from Raphael, Bri acknowledged Philip, her mind still in a fog. "Uh huh, yeah, okay, I'll be right there." She turned back to the wondering gaze of Raphael's entrancement. "Are you going to be okay?"

Raphael seemed to be shaken out of his own spell then. "No doubt," his smooth voice grooved. "Thank you for your kindness. I haven't had a hug like that in..." He thought carefully about the period of time it had been, then realized, "...ever," he said, completely taken aback by the blast of hyperawareness rocketing through his system. Intense. Chilling.

"Oh." Bri frowned slightly, her heart feeling weighed down by the melancholy of his isolation.

Maybe you could help him with that.

The thought jarred her, and she felt more ashamed than she'd ever been in her life.

"Well, if you're ever in need of another one—" she pointed to herself with a tiny smile hinting at the corners of her full lips, "I'm your girl." The chuckle that slipped from her throat was half merriment and half embarrassment. Was she doing too much or was this okay for him? It's all she cared about in that instant.

Raphael's guttural tone simmered across her flesh. "Thank you again. I may hold you to it." He cleared his throat as if he, too, was a little weirded out by their undeniable attraction.

Bri licked her lips. "Well," she rubbed her hands down

the side of her hips just to give her limbs something to do, "I should go see what this emergency is about, and I'll come back around if that's okay."

Raphael nodded with a tilt of his head. "That's very generous of you but not necessary. You're busy, do your thing."

He reached out to Bri before his mind caught up with his movements to stop him from touching her. The fluid caress against her shoulder sent an attack of rippling chills coursing through Bri's veins. They both felt it, and as if it was too much on his senses, Raphael took one step back, then two, before turning to retreat altogether.

That day, Bri circled back around to check on him, but Raphael was nowhere to be found. Afterward, the only other occasion she'd gotten an eyeful of him was at Hunter and Camilla's wedding, then their reception, and a few days later, at a so-called blind date at a galleria with Allison and Lance Valentine.

"You did what?!" Bri had shouted at her best friend, unbelieving that she'd been put in a face-off situation that could end badly.

Allison shushed her. "Is it necessary to be so loud?"

Bri grabbed her friend's wrist and pulled her to a more discreet corner of the galleria. Lowering her voice, Bri's eyes skipped around the museum, then she whispered harshly, "You know good and well I don't like blind dates. What were you thinking?!"

Allison sighed. "I was thinking, you didn't have to look at this like a blind date. It's not like you've never met the guy. Besides, I caught you two staring at one another on more than one occasion."

Bri tossed her hands up spiritedly. "Well, I had to look at him. He was a part of the wedding party!"

"Would you stop freaking out, please?" Allison said.

It was easy for Allison to be all calm and collected when Allison went into the night knowing what would come out of it. Bri, on the other hand, was ruffled to the core. Sure, she wanted to see Raphael again, but Bri knew the brother was broken, and the last thing she could handle was a man who needed therapy or healing because of a terrible past. There was no telling how deep of a psychological trauma his fiancée's death had on him or if he was even capable of moving forward into a relationship.

Besides that, Bri could sense the emotional state of people to the point of drowning in their sorrows or happiness or joy. It was the life of being an empath.

Still, that day, Bri self-consciously took a hand down her clinging blue knee-length dress, readying herself for their *date*.

When Raphael arrived at Lance's side, his flowing gaze lingered on Bri, his curled lashes and dark stare detaining her throughout the night. They'd shared little to no intimate details with each other, only hanging side by side while speaking about the paintings in the galleria whilst trying to ignore the incendiary chemistry that remained between them. It only ended up making them more curious about one another, but instead of exploring that idea, they both maintained a quiet, casual conversation.

The end of the night didn't come suddenly. Bri followed

along as the time ticked by, contemplating if she and Raphael could go somewhere and have a real tête-à-tête. But he'd beaten her to the proverbial punch by declining before she could ask.

It wasn't until weeks later at Northwestern Memorial Hospital did Bri's and Raphael's paths cross yet again. While out for lunch, Camilla's water broke, and she was quickly transported to prep for delivery. As the Valentines waited with anticipation, Bri was huddled in the labor and delivery lobby along with them. The downtime was a lengthy one, and it wasn't until Bri was awakened in the dimly lit room that she realized she'd succumbed to slumber.

Her eyes fluttered opened, adjusting to the chocolate-covered image that squatted before her, with a soft piercing gaze that stayed focused on her. A neatly groomed beard connected to a thin mustache over lush lips stood out in her vision. She blinked once, then twice, but the image still held there. Bri immediately assumed she was dreaming, and to shake herself from the hallucination, she reached out and touched his face, feeling the mixture of soft and roughness through his beard.

He didn't move, but she felt him quiver as if her touch prompted something uninhibited inside him, the same something that wrecked her emotions since their hug at Hunter and Camilla's rehearsal dinner eight months ago. Her fingers skipped up the side of his smooth face where she took a hand over the waves of his low-cut hair. This time, a full shudder expelled from Raphael, and his eyes closed as his hand ran to greet hers almost immediately.

"*Aies pitié*," his dark voice whispered, begging her for mercy.

Bri's eyes popped as she realized this wasn't a dream at all.

"Oh my God," Bri said, feeling bashful. "Raphael, I'm so sorry, I...I thought I was dreaming." She blushed. "Silly me."

Raphael's gaze dropped to her lips, and he forced his sight back to the dark brown of her irises. "Do you dream of me often?" he asked, teasing her.

A wide smile crept across Bri's face, and she tucked her head and covered her eyes with her free hand.

"Um...uh..."

Raphael smirked, almost pleased that he had invaded her fantasies.

"Just tell me I'm looking and smelling good when we meet there."

This brought a chuckle from Bri that made her ears tingle, and her nipples soar as they hardened.

She was surely smitten with him, but Bri still tried to tell herself not to take his kindness for something else.

Be careful with him. It became her mantra to make sure she kept her head on straight. However, that fell right through the door after Raphael invited her to pick up dinner. Their ride to gather the food for all who waited at the hospital was a fulfilling one regardless of the simple tone of the conversation.

"So, you speak French?" she asked, remembering the first thing he spoke when Bri caressed his head after thinking she was dreaming.

He grinned. "Being around the globe at any given time had its perks. I learn the language of the land I visited. Connected with the people."

Bri nodded. "That has to be amazing."

"It was."

Noticing the past tense, Bri hesitated then asked, "Don't you enjoy those same pleasures anymore?"

The shift in his demeanor happened in stages as if the memory of his choices were muddied by an unpleasant recollection.

"Nah." Raphael glanced at her then back to the road. "Those days are gone."

Bri knew there was a more in-depth conversation in this direction, but she was also sure Raphael wouldn't be willing to share it with her now. She wondered if ever a time would come, then quickly remembered her mantra.

Be careful with him.

"Would you like to talk about it?" she heard herself asking.

Silence filled the vehicle. "Maybe some other time."

Bri rubbed her lips together. "Fun fact," she said, deciding to switch gears. "When I was in high school, I took up French and passed with flying colors." She wiggled her brows at him, and Raphael's face lit up.

"So, you can speak the language?"

"Not really." She laughed. "I haven't put it to much use. Maybe you could teach me sometime."

That was how Bri ended up here, at L'ÉCOLE FRANÇAISE. It would've been easier to start these sessions at the beginning of the year—new year, new things and all—but on Christmas, during the wedding reception of Allison and his brother Lance Valentine, Raphael went out in search of Bri, finding her rushing from the ladies' room where she collided with his chest.

"Raphael," she said, "I'm so sorry, please excuse me. I wasn't paying attention."

"You're all right," he said, "I was actually just looking for you. Is there anything I can help with?"

"Oh, um…" Her eyes darted around then went back to him. "No, I think I've got everything covered."

"Just like the superwoman you are," he said with a handsome smile. "Somehow, I knew you'd say that."

Bri blushed. "Yes, well, it's my thing, ya know."

Raphael nodded. "I do know, and you do it quite well, I might add." Raphael paused. "You know we never had the chance to exchange numbers, and I've wondered if you were still up for visiting St. Louis with me."

Not only did they make plans for French lessons with one another during that intense ride to pick up food, but they'd also made plans to visit the other side of his family in St. Louis.

Bri acquiesced immediately, and as Allison spoke into the microphone about the ladies coming up for the bouquet tossing, Bri and Raphael noticed they were standing underneath a sprig of mistletoe. The seconds between the realization had both of their hearts beating and pulses thumping. For Raphael, years had passed since he kissed a woman, but something about the nudge in his heart made him ask a question.

"May I?"

A blush layered Bri's cheeks, and she nodded as she responded on a breathless whisper. "Yes."

He stepped forward, slipping a slow-moving arm around her snatched waist to pull Bri into the sanctuary of his solid torso.

The masculine scent he carried wafted around them as if sealing their bodies together while Raphael dropped his lips to hers, his mouth spreading the soft flesh of her rims as he buried his lips in consolidation with her own. An inferno covered them in perpetual allure, sinking into their skin and stoking an already burning fire that threatened to knock them over. Desire streamed through their bodies, and when Raphael's tongue traced the inner edges of Bri's lips, she opened to him and was taken by the strong wrestling of his wet muscle as his tongue dived inside her mouth.

Sparks like she'd never felt before attacked her entire being, and her breathing hitched into overdrive as her body melted into his.

It had taken extreme focus to detached themselves from one another, then suddenly, out of nowhere Bri was hit on the side of her head with Allison's bouquet of roses. Bri's heart had never thumped so recklessly. What was really going on?

Unsure, she stared at Raphael as he bent down and lifted the flowers to her.

"I believe these belong to you."

Bri couldn't blink, move, or respond. Her heart hammered fiercely in her chest. The pandemonium was so out of control she was sure to fall over at any moment.

However, she snapped out of it when Allison rushed to their sides, squealing.

"Oh my God, I can't believe you caught it!"

Bri was still staring at Raphael, but she blinked over at Allison in a daze, trying to clear her head.

Allison continued to squeal as Lance, Xavier, Hunter, Kyle, DeAndre, and their father Leslie crowded around with hinting smiles and devilish grins.

They pulled Raphael away who couldn't seem to tear his all-encompassing gaze apart from Bri's. Before the night ended, Raphael made sure to exchange numbers, and two days later, Bri found herself at L'ÉCOLE FRANÇAISE, with Raphael as the teacher and Bri St. James as the student.

The saucer of strawberries sat in front of her as she lifted one to her lips and bit into the juicy fruit.

"Mmmm. That's sweet," she said. "Soft and juicy, too."

Raphael grinned, the spread of his delicious mouth making her pulse thump.

"I picked them up on the way over from the fresh food market on Twenty-Ninth and Malcolm."

"Oh, their fruit is always the freshest. Do you shop there all the time?"

"Only for my fruit."

"Me, too," she said.

Bri reached for another strawberry, but Raphael eased the saucer back across the table to rest in front of him.

"Heeeey, I wasn't done with that."

Raphael chuckled. "Say that in *français*, and you can have another."

Bri twisted her lips and pouted, and Raphael's heavy chuckle warmed her from within.

"It's impossible," she said.

Raphael's tongue traced his bottom lip. "Not only is it possible, but if you get it right, you can have the last five."

Bri's eyes widened slightly. "You don't play fair, Mr. Valentine."

Raphael laughed again. "Come on," he said. "Repeat after me. We went over a few basic words. Remember, I is *je* in *français*. What you must consider is some words change slightly when they're put together in a sentence. Whereas wasn't would normally be *n'était pas*, when used in a sentence such as this, it would be *n'avais pas*. Not much of a difference but a slight change nonetheless."

Bri nodded. "Okay, I can do this."

"*Je n'avais pas fini avec ça.*"

Raphael gave her the sentence once, then watched her mouth as she practiced the words in a whisper before speaking them out loud. He ignored the stir in his gut and the fast pace of his heart as he tried to focus on the lesson.

Squaring her shoulders and lifting her chin, Bri spoke, "*Je n'avais pas fini avec ça.*"

Raphael's gaze twinkled, and his lips grew into an awestruck smile.

"*Parfait!*" he exclaimed.

Bri clapped her hands merrily. "That means perfect, right? I got that right, right?" she asked excitedly.

Raphael nodded, reveling in her rejoicing while still trying to ignore the tap dancing of his heart. "Yes, you did, and it came out with a fluent flow. You'll be a pro in no time, *amour*," his thick voice strummed.

"Eeee!" Bri continued to clap excitedly, and Raphael slid the saucer of strawberries back across the table.

"Would you like some? I'm willing to share." She smiled over at him while biting down into the soft fruit.

Raphael forced his gaze from the fullness of her lips.

"Nah, go ahead, you earned them."

"Are you sure?" she asked in a muffled tone. "Oops!" She cupped her mouth as juice slid from the corner of her lips.

Raphael followed the trickle down her chin, and the unencumbered arousal in his pants jarred him. He stood to his full height and glanced down at his watch.

"This place will be closing soon. We should probably wrap this up."

His nerves were rattled, but Bri didn't seem to notice. She nodded, also standing after she polished off all but one strawberry. With the fruit in one hand and the saucer in the other, Bri rounded the table to stand in front of him.

"Please," she said, "I insist."

She held the fruit to his lips, and his heartbeat crashed when her nearness found its way in between the breadth of his chest. Without further delay Raphael opened his mouth, mistakenly sucking in her finger that had been holding the fruit at elevation.

A tsunami of unrestrained chills soared through them both. Raphael tasted the sweetness of her flesh and fruit while Bri was bracketed with a ripple of heat. She almost cursed but fought the profanity in a quick close of her mouth to lock her jaw. Raphael's tongue cruised over his lips as he folded his mouth together.

Bri cleared her throat. "Nothing like fresh fruit from the marketplace, huh? They're number one in the sweet ripeness, I think." Her husky voice came out in a purr. Then she attempted to clear her throat, noting the sultriness of her vocals.

"I'm not sure," he said. "I'm thinking they may be running a close second."

Bri eyed him a moment. He wasn't suggesting what she thought, was he?

"A close second to?"

His heavy gaze traveled over her, then he nodded in her direction. "You."

Bri swallowed back a lump in her throat, and her heartbeat tapped a wild dance in her chest. She blushed as heat filled her face and more chills settled in the base of her belly.

Raphael couldn't explain what happened next. It was as if something other than he commanded his body. He took one step that erased the gap between them and slipped a hand around her neck, dropping his mouth to her lips. Bri gasped and welcomed the warm feel of his mouth as her eyes closed and her lips parted.

A flame filled her panties, almost knocking her over as Raphael stole her mouth and sucked her tongue.

The saucer in her hand was forgotten, and it crashed to the granite floor, breaking on impact. The shatter of it disassembled Raphael's flow, and he jerked from Bri's mouth, eyes wide and breath hitched.

"Shit," he mumbled. "*Amour*, please, forgive me, I don't usually—"

"No, please, don't apologize. I rather enjoyed it." She smiled coyly and dropped her gaze from his to the saucer pieces on the floor. "My goodness, I've made a mess."

Bri squatted to clean it up just as Raphael did, his hand covering hers as she reached for the broken pieces.

"Don't worry," he said. "It's my mess to clean."

They stared at each other longingly. And instead of moving away, they both cleared the floor, then quietly left the class headed for the garage.

At Bri's car, Raphael opened the driver door and helped her inside the Mercedes Benz. She adjusted her bottom in the seat, then turned over her engine and powered down her window.

Slipping his hands inside his pockets, Raphael stared down at her then nodded and spoke. "Seatbelt."

"Oh, yeah, of course." Her hands fumbled for the strap, crossing it over her chest, then glanced back at him. "Better?"

"Much."

They smiled.

"I had a good time today. I feel like I'll be speaking *français* in no time."

He loved the spread of her mouth as she beamed, and in turn, bit down on his lip. An exhale left him, then Raphael spoke. "You will. I'll make sure of it."

Bri lifted a brow. "What if I become one of those students that's hard to teach, huh?" She wiggled her brow playfully.

"Then we'll have to find a better way for you to compre-hend." He paused for a long minute. "I can think of a thing or two that may get you going."

Bri's smile fell as a shudder rocked through her body.

"When you get home, call or text to let me know you made it there safely."

Bri nodded, her voice lost.

"*Amour*," he said as a final goodbye. Raphael took a few steps back, giving Bri the room to pull away.

She did, unhurriedly, trying to shake herself from their connection. It was no secret to herself that Bri was falling in like with Raphael. One could argue that it was too late, actually. She liked him, a lot.

Now what to do with that, she wasn't sure. The jury, was still, in deliberation.

Chapter Two

*L*ater that night, Bri's mind was in a fog as she washed the three dishes and two utensils in her sink. Her downtown studio apartment was her saving grace when she stepped out on a limb to open Building Bridges Wedding and Event Planning, a company she founded in the 1990s. But now the space seemed as if it had shrunken, and Bri was considering relocating.

"But it's cold outside," she whined to herself, shuddering with just the thought of moving in Chicago's frigid temperatures.

She could wait till summer, but that was half a year away, and by that time, Bri felt she would be living in a box. A sigh escaped her, then Bri recognized she'd been washing the same dish in circles for minutes. Pursing her lips with a squint of her eyes, Bri dried the plate with a hand towel then added it to her cabinet.

The phone on the mini island chirped, and she sauntered over to it and answered it on the first ring.

"Aren't you supposed to be on your honeymoon?"

On the other end, Allison Valentine smiled and rolled across a large memory foam platform bed.

"I am on my honeymoon, but Lance left the villa to grab some ice, so I thought I would check in on you."

"You mean you wanted to be nosy and get in my business."

"Oh, you have business now?" A sharp squealing cackle left Allison's mouth.

"You're really funny, you know that?"

Allison nodded with tears spilling from the corners of her lids. "I think it was pretty humorous, don't you?"

"Hardly."

Allison's laugh traveled through the phone, and Bri pulled the receiver from her ear and cut her eyes at it.

"Now you're just having too much fun," Bri added.

"No, seriously," Allison said, wiping the moisture from her face. "What's going on with you and Raphael? Are you guys a thing? Is this really happening?"

Bri sighed. "You're moving too fast for me, girl. Raphael and I are just friends. Nothing more, nothing less."

Allison scoffed. "Please save me the denial, okay. I, along with everyone else at our wedding party, witnessed that kiss between you two, and honey, let me be the one to tell you if no one has already," Bri half-rolled her eyes, "the way he pulled you into that embrace and kissed your mouth, a running semi couldn't break you-all's connection...." Allison smacked her lips. "Shidddd. Nothing about it was a 'just-friends' kiss. Raphael has a thing for you, and I didn't need to tell you that for you to know it."

Bri's blank gaze transformed into a blush, and a grin was etched at the corner of her mouth.

"Allison, you know just as well as I do that Raphael isn't ready for a relationship." Her gaze drifted off to the sofa a few feet away. "He may never be," she whispered.

Allison scoffed again. "Yeah, I would've believed that a few months ago, but now, I'm not so sure."

"And you got all of that because of a kiss?"

"Bri, that was not just any kiss. Okay, let's make a deal. If you guys find yourselves together again, and another kiss happens, promise me you'll admit that you two have a thing for each other."

Bri sucked in her lips and thought of the kiss she received from him earlier. His mouth had been warm, inviting, soft, and firm simultaneously. A mild vibration rippled through Bri as her mind reminisced, so deep in the memory, she could smell his manly fragrance.

"Hello, did I lose you?"

Bri blinked rapidly. "No, I, um…I'm still here."

"Well don't get quiet on me now. I need answers before Lance gets back."

"I don't have the info you're looking for, friend. And I'm not sure when I'll see Raphael again."

"Well, do you have plans for New Year's Eve?"

"No, not really."

"What does that mean? Do you or don't you?"

"I don't, but I was thinking of attending a masquerade ball happening at the Drake Hotel."

"That's an excellent way to bring in the new year," Allison squealed. "Why don't you invite Raphael?"

Bri thought it over, and a smile pulled at her lips. "I don't want to pressure him, you know."

"Girl, please. This is a grown man we're talking about. If he's not into it, I'm sure he'll say as much. Don't you trust him to at least speak his mind or tell you the truth?"

Bri was silent, her heart kicking up a fuss as she thought of being arm in arm with Raphael at the masquerade party.

"I'll ask him and see what he says, but Allison, if this backfires, I'm coming for you."

"Oh, honey, I'm a million miles away, so I'm not scared."

Bri rolled her eyes as Allison chuckled. "That's not funny. You don't know what type of anxieties Raphael may be dealing with when it comes to his late-fiancée."

"Girl, you make it sound like the man is haunted."

"He may be."

"Listen, you're somewhat right. He could have some unresolved issues, but again, he couldn't be all that troubled with the way he smacked on those lips the other day. But anyway, I'll respect your decision. I'm not here to push you. I can just see you two together, and maybe it's the love in the air that makes me want to fight for you guys."

Bri nodded. "Let's just start slow all right? I'll ask him to the party, and we'll go from there."

"Riiiiight. So you are feeling him, then?"

Bri pursed her lips and leaned into a hip. "Are you playing with me?"

Allison chuckled. "Just a little bit."

"You should focus on your honeymoon."

"Oh, babe, trust me when I tell you I'm not distracted."
She snickered. "We simply had an intermission."

"So, what's the ice for, or do I want to know?"

"Now, that, ain't none of your business."

"Oh, but all of your questions about me and Raphael
is yours?"

"Yeah. I'm his sister now, and you're my best friend. I'm
rooting for both of you."

"Yeah, yeah. Have fun in…wait, where are you guys?"

Allison blushed. "Grenada at the Levera Nature and
Beach Resort."

"Oooh, I'm jealous."

Allison giggled. "Aww, don't be." Allison paused. "Oops,
I gotta go, girl. My man is back."

"They did have handcuffs. We're in luck," Lance's voice
drummed through the phone.

Bri's eyes lurched. "Handcuffs!" she shrieked. "I thought
he was going to get ice?"

Allison's voice was muffled, and Bri could hear smacking
and squeals from the other end.

"I'm just going to hang up." Bri ended the call and
stared at the phone a moment before shaking off the ripple
that slipped through her. Everyone seemed to be in love and
getting some action but her. She blew out a sigh and left the
phone on the table as she strolled around the mini isle to the
tiny space that contained her desk.

Sitting down, her eyes traveled over to the time while her
hand waved across the wireless mouse—six-thirty-five p.m.
The monitor lit up, then Bri typed in her password and

worked across the screen to check the daily reports with Building Bridges Wedding and Event Planning. This was something she did a few times a month, just to make sure things were on the up and up, and nothing was awry.

However, after logging into the business account, Bri stiffened as her eyes sailed across two balances. One that said Available, and the other underlined with red. She frowned.

"What is this?" Bri murmured.

Clicking the red line brought a notice onto the screen.

Blocked Funds. Please call 800…

Bri sat back against her swivel chair in disbelief. Her thoughts shuffled before she stood and headed back to the mini isle where she retrieved her phone and dashed back to her desk to dial the number in question.

As she waited for a representative to answer the phone, her mind failed to come up with a reasonable explanation. Why would there be funds blocked in her business account?

"Thank you for calling Merriam Bank, this is Seth Jackson, how can I assist you today?"

The representative sounded as if his nose was clogged, and before Bri could speak, the man sneezed.

"Achoo!" He sniffled. "Oh my God, I'm so sorry, please excuse me. I caught a cold from my three-year-old. Apparently, half of the kids in his class caught a virus while on a field trip." The man chuckled, though he sounded miserable.

"I'm sorry to hear that. Do you need to pass me along to someone else?"

"No, no, no, I can help you with whatever you need."

"That's refreshing because I need someone who can tell me why there are funds in my account frozen."

"Let me have your account number, name, and verify your password for me."

Bri rattled off the information as Seth's fingers worked the keyboard in front of him. He hummed a bit as he waited for the data to pop up, but Bri's eyes were focused on the monitor before her.

"Oh…" Seth said after a moment longer.

"What does that mean?"

A rustling in the pit of Bri's stomach made her lock her jaw as she suddenly became worried.

"I've got a number for you to call." He rattled off the number, and Bri quickly grabbed an ink pen, scribbling it across a notepad next to her mouse.

"What is this?"

Seth was quiet a moment more. "Let me confirm something real quick. Do you mind if I put you on a brief hold?"

Hell yeah, she minded. Bri wanted to know just what in the world was going on, and Seth was too discreet for her taste. She wasn't quick enough to refuse his request to hold, and elevator music sounded through the receiver. Bri scoffed and glanced at the phone as if Seth had lost his mind. A few agonizing minutes of waiting, and Seth returned.

"Thank you for your patience."

"Tell me what's going on with my account." Bri's matter-of-fact tone was all business and matter-of-fact.

"Yes, ma'am. It appears as if the IRS has placed a hold for the funds in your account."

Bri's mouth dropped on a gasp. "What?!"

"It's not your entire account balance but a partial amount."

"Partial?! First, two hundred and thirty-five thousand dollars and seventy-nine cents is not just a partial amount. It's a load of money. Secondly, this is bizarre since I pay my taxes quarterly every year!"

"Yes, I understand your frustration. Unfortunately, there's nothing I can do about it or anyone else at this institution. You would need to call the IRS."

Bri cursed profusely, annoyed that this was happening right now.

"Thank you, Seth, goodbye."

She disconnected the line as Seth tried to complete his ending call speech. In complete astonishment, Bri sat for a second, her mind swirling at the thought that she could owe taxes. The money was taken from the business account every quarter on time. She had receipt of payments made that were given to her by...

"No..." she whispered. Her mind wandered to Philip Daniels, her photographer, and business partner.

Bri and Philip met during their sophomore year at Clark Atlanta University. They crossed paths when two of their classes intercepted one another. Both were natives of Chicago and in the field of design, the two gravitated toward each other, partnering during assignments and studying when it came down to preparing for a test.

However, halfway through his studies, Philip decided what he wanted to make a career as a photographer. Bri urged him on, stating, "You could work for me when it's all said and done."

Philip peered at her. "Work for you?"

"Well, not like my employee or anything. We could be partners."

Philip nodded at the idea. "So we would share fifty percent of the company?"

Bri's eyes rolled as she thought for a minute. "I wouldn't say fifty-fifty. I plan to own a wedding planning business. I already have a business license. Have for years. It just took me a while to put a plan into action. I'll be all right with sharing a piece of it, so you don't feel like you're working for me but not fifty percent."

Philip rubbed his jaw. Naturally, he would've objected because he too wanted to run his own business. However, he could still have a separate photography gig and be part owner of another. It would give him experience fresh out of college and make his resume more reputable.

"How much are we talking here?"

"Thirty percent," she stated.

It didn't take long for Philip to think it over. "Let's shake on it." He held out his hand, and Bri accepted it.

Bri was thrilled. That was one less contractor she would need to hire to help with her company. To make matters more exceptional, he was business savvy, and she could trust him to have the company's best interest at heart since he owned a piece.

Now sitting in front of her monitor with her mind boggled with the possibility that Philip had not been paying the taxes, Bri inhaled and exhaled deeply, rattled to her core.

"Okay, don't jump to conclusions. There has to be a

good explanation for this." She rose from the chair and walked to her purse, retrieving her keys and coat then headed for the front door. "I'm sure this is all a misunderstanding, and Philip will have the paperwork necessary to prove our payments." Bri nodded, certain her mess would be untangled soon.

She left her studio apartment in a rush to head for Daniels Photography; she *would* get answers about the trouble that had just landed on their doorstep.

Chapter Three

"*P*lease tell me there's an explanation for this."

After marching in his office and pulling Philip out of his desk chair, Bri took over his computer and pulled up the bank account showing the frozen assets. She stared up at his coffee brown face into light brown eyes that shifted away from her.

"I can explain."

Bri's belly wrestled with fear. "No," she shook her head, "you are not about to tell me that the receipts I have that show we pay taxes every quarter aren't real." Her head continued to shake. "Please. Tell me it's not what you're about to say."

"It's not."

Bri breathed a tiny sigh of relief, but still, there was a clench in her gut that made her brace for more.

"Not exactly, anyway," he said.

"What is going on, Philip?"

He clasped his hands together, his fingers working around a closed fist nervously.

"Okay, I should've told you this long ago, but I was trying to resolve the issue on my own without your involvement."

"Yeah, well, now I'm involved, so get straight to the point." Her fear was turning into anger, and she wrestled to keep her temper restrained.

"When I first started my photography business, I didn't quite have what was needed for upfront costs. Originally, I went over the plans and researched the income I would need, but when it was time to pull it all together, I was short." He paused, and his attention shifted from hers to the wall, to his hand, then back to her face. When their eyes met again, apprehension filled his gaze.

"I took some of the tax money and used it to complete the funding of Daniels Photography." He rushed to add, "but I have been sending the IRS payments," he paused again, "I just missed the last two, so now they're trying to put a hold on our account."

For the longest time, Bri was silent. She stared at the face she once considered to be one of her favorites. Their relationship was platonic in every aspect, like brother and sister, for the five years of their acquaintance. There was never a reason to distrust him, but hearing him now put a vile taste in her mouth.

"So, instead of you coming to me and saying, hey Bri I could really use your help with something, you went behind my back and stole money from the business. Is that right?"

Philip sighed exasperatedly. "I didn't steal it; as I said—"

"You did!" Bri shouted. She held her finger out, pointing at him as more anger rose within her. "When you take money that doesn't belong to you, it's called stealing!"

Philip inhaled deeply in a lean, his shoulders rising as he huffed.

"Okay, you know what, you're right. I'm sorry. I never meant for it to get out of hand."

Bri locked her jaw and shook her head. She hated to feel this disgust.

"Philip, it's been four years since I officially opened this business." She held a hand up with four fingers. "*Quatre!*" she shouted, speaking the number in French. "So you mean to tell me, all of this time, the payments haven't been up to date?" Bri didn't give him a chance to respond before she shouted. "I trusted you!" Her breathing became ragged.

"Listen, Bri, please, I know it looks bad, but I can fix this. I'm going to fix this."

Bri shut her eyes and tried to calm her spirit, but she was officially rattled, and everything she thought about Philip being honest and trustworthy, disappeared with the knowledge he had misled her.

He reached for her shoulder, and she pulled away. "You lied to me, with a straight face, for four years?"

Bri's heart was broken. Philip was one of the good guys in her eyes. She wished his dreams would come true and that he would try and make room for a love he couldn't live without at some point. But he'd worked tirelessly, claiming when it was time for that, it would happen.

Bri was certain one day he would make someone happy

and, on top of that, have the means to support his family. Like a little sister, she pushed him, encouraging him to open his photography business. Could it be possible that her pushing was too much? Was she just as responsible for this as he?"

She shook her head, disturbed and needing to get some fresh air. Without another word, Bri sidestepped him and headed to the door.

"It's not a million dollars. You're overreacting," he said, spinning to face her retreating back.

Bri halted her steps and twirled on her heels with eyebrows that frowned.

"I'm overreacting?" She couldn't believe it, and now her confusion had risen into anger again. "Two hundred and thirty-five thousand dollars and seventy-nine cents is nothing to sneeze at! Are you crazy!?"

"Baby, your company is worth a little over five million now, you can't be stressing about two hundred thous—"

"Wait a minute, back up." She gave him a stern eye, her mind shuffling to make sure she'd understood him. "Did you just call me 'baby'?"

Philip closed his mouth and locked his jaw. Bri knew she had heard him right, but still, she couldn't help but wait for an answer as she folded her arms across her chest.

"It slipped out, you're missing my point."

"Oh, I don't think I am. You apparently believe it's not that big of a deal to manipulate your business partner. I thought you were better than that?"

"I am! Come on, Bri!"

"No!" she shouted. "You come on, Philip! It's easy to say

it's just two-hundred thousand dollars when it isn't your money you're playing with! How dare you! I just won the first annual WedStyle award! I'm going to be featured in *Premier Bride Magazine*! Building Bridges Wedding and Event Planning—owned by an African-American woman—is on its way to becoming a household name four years after its opening! The last thing I need is for some news outlet to get hold of information like this! I'm in the public eye! Everything I've worked hard for is in jeopardy because it looks like I don't pay my taxes, Philip! How dare you!"

Her anger was bubbling over.

"I thought this was our business," he said.

Bri's head suddenly thumped with an ache.

"Are you kidding me? That's what you have to say, after everything I just pointed out?"

"I'm just saying you're not the only one on the line."

"And who put us there?" Her eyes were wide, her breathing hitched. "You said you didn't want to be a part of the 'show,' as you called it. It's not your name or face currently being recognized." She bit her lip and shook her head. "You know what. You're out!"

Philips brows knocked together. "What does that mean?"

"I'm buying you out! The thirty percent you own, it's mine!"

"You can't do that."

"I can and I will. Sell it to me, or I'm getting the best lawyer money can buy and suing your ass for embezzlement."

Philip's eyes widened. "You wouldn't."

Bri leaned into a hip, her arms still crossed as she stared into his face.

"Don't do this. I love this company just as much as you."

"Yeah, well, you have a great way of showing it."

Bri spun on her heels so incensed that she couldn't stand to be in his presence another second.

"Bri, we need to talk about this," he said at her back. But Bri continued her departure, opening the door and slamming it on her way out.

OUTSIDE IN HER CAR, BRI RESTED HER HEAD AGAINST THE seat with her eyes closed as she murmured a steady chant.

"Calm down, Bri. Everything's gonna be okay. Pull it together."

She tried with all the strength inside her to bring her anger down so she could think with a clear head, but it was hard to do, especially since the matter at stake needed to be handled immediately.

Bri needed someone to talk to. Someone who would listen and give her sound advice. Her mind went to Allison, but she shook the thought since Bri didn't want to interrupt Allison's honeymoon.

"But this is an emergency," she said to herself, fishing for the cell phone at the bottom of her purse. Clutching it in her grasp, Bri paused again, then dropped her head back against the seat with a sigh of reluctance. It would be selfish to call.

"Damn it," she cursed.

Blowing out a stream of air, Bri's mind jogged in circles. Philip was the closest thing to a best friend beside Allison. Bri didn't have many people to consult with. Unless she called her parents. Bri bit her bottom lip as her mind traveled to Raphael.

He would listen to her. At least, that's what she thought, but would it be premature to bombard him with her problems? They were still getting to know each other, and she didn't want to scare the poor guy off. Bri begin to nibble on her lip just as the phone in her hand kicked out a jingle.

Bri glanced down. It was Raphael. A flutter in her chest followed by a rumbling in her stomach gave Bri pause. What was that? Nervousness? Excitement? Or both? Without thinking too long on it, she answered the call.

"Hello?" Her voice was hitched, an uncertainty mixed with surprise and frustration.

"Did I catch you at a bad time?"

The dark groove of his voice sent chills spreading over her skin. How was she instantly turned on and the man had only asked her a question?

Bri shut her eyes and exhaled longingly as if she'd been holding her breath until this very moment. "No, I was just thinking about you." She cleared her throat.

Raphael, too, could hear the unease in her voice. "I'm not in trouble, am I?"

Bri smiled softly and dipped her head, then rubbed her lips together.

"No. It's all me."

Raphael was silent for a second while Bri fidgeted with what to tell him if anything at all.

"I know it's me that called you, but I sense you have something on your mind. Feels substantial. Why don't you tell me about it?" He asked.

Another flutter rippled through Bri, and this time, the wave of energy covered her completely. She relaxed in the comfort of his attention.

"Is that why you called, to find out what was wrong with me?" Bri teased. "No, of course not," she answered without giving him a chance to. "How would you have known?" It was now Bri's thoughts that escaped her head only to manifest in words off her tongue. "Excuse me, I must sound like a rambling idiot."

"I would never compare an idiot to the likings of you, *amour*."

Bri shut her eyes again, another exhale, leaving her mouth on a long string of wind. She had to get her thoughts together, or she would remain poised in the comfort of hearing him breathe through the receiver.

"Raphael, I'm in a bit of a pickle, and I know what I'm about to ask may be something you can't help me with, and if that's the case, I'm perfectly okay with that." She paused. "Damn it, I'm rambling again." Bri rolled her eyes and closed her mouth.

"Are you stuck somewhere, do you need a ride?" He asked. "It was my initial reason for calling."

Bri could've smacked herself upside the head. Of course. Raphael mentioned before they departed earlier for Bri to reach out to him once she'd made it safely home. Hours later, she hadn't, and being the gentleman he was, calling to check on her was a no-brainer.

"Oh no, my car is fine, I'm sorry." She inhaled another long breath. "I'm sitting inside of it now, trying to get my thoughts together. I was going to call you, but I became distracted."

"What's wrong?"

"Um, well, I'm in a bit of a bind, and I need a photographer for a wedding in two weeks. Is there any way you would be willing to be my stand-in guy? I promise to pay you accordingly. Whatever your price, that is."

Bri bit down on her lips with a squint as she braced for his response, but his silence stretched for so long that she assumed he was no longer there.

"Hello, are you still there?"

"Yes," he said. "It's been a while since I've done a public event."

"I know, and I'm so sorry to ask you this." She paused. "You know what, never mind. I will find someone on short notice."

"You know?" Raphael asked.

"What?"

"You said, you know it's been a while since I've done a public event."

Bri was silent as she thought it over. "Yeah."

"How do you know that?"

Busted.

"Um, well, I..." She fumbled with her words. "I researched you." Bri closed her eyes again, feeling like the idiot she'd just claimed to be. How she'd let that slip out eluded her. But it was too late to take the words back now.

"I see."

"It wasn't to pry, I was just intrigued. I apologize if that makes you feel uncomfortable."

Raphael chuckled. "You sound nervous. There's no need to be. I looked you up, too."

That revelation surprised Bri, and her eyes enlarged as a smirk settled at the corners of her lips.

"Why? I'm not that interesting."

"I stand to disagree, *amour*. You are very intriguing to me."

Bri bit down on her lip, her lashes fluttering as a blush surfaced on her face.

"Have breakfast with me," Raphael said.

"Now?" Bri glanced at the time. It was nearly eight at night.

"*Pas de jolie dame...le matin.*"

Bri slowly interpreted his words in her head. *No, pretty lady...in the morning.*

Her cheeks took on an innate shadow of brown as she blushed again.

"I understood you," she said wistfully.

"*Excusez-moi?*"

Bri giggled. "I said, *je t'ai...*" She paused and thought over the pronunciation. "*Je t'ai compris.*" She smirked, wondering if she'd just butchered *I understood you*, or if it came out like it was supposed to.

"Very nice, *amour*, you learn quickly."

"Thanks." Her smile was full force now, spreading across her face as if it was the highlight of her day.

"So, in the morning, you can tell me what's going on

with you, and in the meantime, I'll check my schedule to see if I can help you with your wedding."

"Really?" Bri was half in shock. Although he hadn't agreed on anything as of yet, getting this far was good enough, and she would take it.

"*Chose sûre.*" Sure thing.

"What time?"

"What works best for you?"

"This time of year," Bri replied, "I'm on the treadmill about six-thirty in the morning, but I prefer outdoor running. For some reason, it's relaxing and a little bit better when the wind is hitting my face. I think it has to do with me running against something that's determined to hold me back. It gives me this willpower to succeed, and I apply that to my life. Is that weird?"

"Not at all. I think I rather like that analogy," he said.

"What about you? What's your morning routine like? I'm sure you're in the gym considering…"

"Considering what?"

He was teasing her, but she kept opening up to his bait.

"Seriously, look at yourself. You have to be every bit of… hmm, if I had to guess, six-three and well over 200 pounds."

"Well over?"

"I didn't mean that in a bad way." She shut her mouth and dipped her head. "Trust me, I did not mean that in any disrespectful type of way. Your body is amazing."

"And you know this by seeing me in my clothes?"

Heat stung her cheeks. It wasn't as if she'd never imagined him without his attire—because she had.

"I could have a beer belly underneath this shirt for all you know."

Bri laughed. "Yeah, I doubt that very seriously."

Raphael's intimate chuckle rippled over her skin, breaking its barrier only to slide a string of heat over her panties.

"How does eight-thirty sound?" He asked.

"Sounds great. Where should I meet you?"

"I would rather pick you up if that's okay."

"Oh, no, that's fine. Do you have something to write my address down with?"

With movement in the background, Bri waited patiently until Raphael responded. "I do now."

She rattled off her address. "I'll be ready at eight-thirty."

"Okay, I'll see you then."

"Yeah, see you."

Bri ended the call, resting her head back against the seat. She hoped for her sake and her client's sake that Raphael's schedule would be free.

Glancing back toward Daniels Photography, Bri sighed, then turned the keys and left for home.

Chapter Four

"**I** loved the movie. It was sweet, romantic, and swoon-worthy."

Raphael glanced at his fiancée Chastity, a smirk lingering at the corners of his mouth. "If you say so," he said.

Chastity gawked, and her face brightened into an exuberant smile. "You didn't like it?"

Raphael held his tongue. The critically acclaimed movie *The Notebook* went back to the big screen on the tenth-year anniversary of its debut. It was all Chastity could talk about seeing from the moment news broke about the novel returning to theaters. And while Raphael enjoyed his time with her at the viewing, he couldn't say that he'd thoroughly enjoyed the cinema.

"It was…different from the romance movies you usually watch."

Chastity folded her arms and puckered her lips. "How do you…" A gasp broke from her mouth, and then her arm reached out and clutched his shoulder. "BABE, watch out!"

Raphael only had a moment to glance back at the road, but when he did, a Dodge Durango crossed the median, en route to hit them head-on. He smashed the brakes, but it was impossible to avoid the collision. With a firm yank on the steering wheel, Raphael swerved to a hard right, his jaw locking as he braced to take on the force of the crash.

The impact locked their seatbelts, and the airbags deployed as the car spun three hundred and sixty degrees before slamming into a guardrail. The engine caught on fire, rising through the damaged hood and growing with each passing second. Both Raphael and Chastity were unconscious, but for a brief moment, Raphael pulled from the haze, dazed, as he glanced to her.

"Chas…" It was only a murmur, barely audible and unheard by Chastity Sinclair. "Sweetheart…" He reached for her slumped body, but the spell carried him back under where connecting with his fiancée was a universe away.

SWEAT SATURATED RAPHAEL'S FACE, CASTING A SHEEN down the column of his neck and the broad length of his shoulders as he sat up in bed. It was happening again. The day his fiancée was taken from him, manifesting in a dream as it had for the past four years when the anniversary of her passing loomed.

Raphael cleared his throat and tossed his legs over the side of the bed where he strolled with long, purposeful

strides through the carpeted master bedroom into the bathroom. There, he slid open the glass shower door, turning the
knob and adjusting the water temperatures for a cool
cascade. He peeled out of his Calvin Klein stretch boxer
briefs and slipped under the spray of the showerhead,
instantly soothed by the drum of falling drops.

A sigh escaped his lips, and with his head down,
Raphael planted his hands outward, bracing one on the
shower wall and the other on the glass door. The strength
in his bulging biceps and shoulders created an appalachian
of rugged hills, that ran across the stretch of his back,
covered in melanin-rich skin. The cool beads were refreshing, but they didn't remove the recollection of that fatal day,
only lightened the memory, as he fought to shake the voice
that screamed his name and the loud screech of metal
to metal.

Raphael's heart beat recklessly, and with his eyes closed,
he murmured, "I'm sorry..."

His jaw locked, and a shudder ran through his vertebrae
just as the memory faded and another resurfaced in
its place.

It was two years after Chastity's death. Raphael was
sitting alone on a sofa in the darkroom that he used to
develop his film. The lights were dimmed as he waited for
the pictures hanging to complete their process, and although
he lingered, Raphael wasn't in a hurry to see the outcome
of their development. The film was the last of the pictures
taken with Chastity, captured in a still moment. Ones he
couldn't bring himself to process before now.

"It should've been me," he murmured simultaneously, in

the flashback and in his current stance under the showerhead.

Raphael's heart continued to beat hurriedly, and in the reminiscence, he moved from the sofa to stand before the first image. His pulse thumped hastily, and his throat tightened as a strain of anxiety fell over him. Raphael took in a deep breath, turning on a mini flashlight that rested in the palm of his hand. He neared the film with it, only casting a shadow across the picture to get his first glimpse of her beautiful face.

But it was not Chastity's face at all reflecting from the picture. His eyes widened, and his mouth parted.

"Bri?"

Snapping out of his reverie, Raphael lifted his head as the water continued to pelt his face. He dropped his arms and took a step back, alarmed that the memory morphed into something else altogether.

Turning the shower knob caused the water to subside, and quickly, Raphael moved from the stall, dripping as he headed for his cell phone. He paid no mind to the trail of water that laid a path behind him. His only aim was to check on Bri and make sure everything was all right.

Making it to his smartphone at record speed, Raphael dialed her number, briefly taking his eye across the time. Four a.m. The phone rang once, twice, three times, and when no answer came, he locked his jaw and internally told himself to calm down. He redialed her number but received the same automatic voicemail.

Disconnecting, Raphael dropped his hand while rubbing the other down his face. He didn't move, only mounted on a ridge of testosterone and strength; overcast in the night's shadow of darkness as he contemplated going to her house. As his thoughts churned, the phone rang, cutting through the silence of his deliberation. He answered without checking the ID.

"Are you all right?" his thick voice drummed.

On the other end of the phone, Bri St. James sat on the edge of her bed, her hair wrapped in a scarf with only the light from a nearby lamp hosting a display of illumination in her space. His question confused her.

"Raphael? Um, yeah…of course." Her brows furrowed. "Are you okay?"

Raphael let go of a rushing breath. Foolish. "I…apologize for waking you." He paused again. "I thought…" Silence lingered, and Bri clutched the phone tighter to her ear as if doing so would dispense the words he held back.

"I'm sorry," he apologized again. "I didn't mean to wake you."

"It's okay. I needed to get up anyway." Bri cleared her throat and glanced back at the clock resting on the nightstand. "But, are you okay?"

The stillness from the other end of the phone made Bri flip the device in her hand to check the screen and make sure he was still there. As the seconds ticked on, she placed it back to her ear just as he spoke.

"I will be. Again, I apologize for disturbing you."

"That's okay. I'd rather be woken up by your warm voice than my alarm shrieking anyway." She chuckled lightly, and the compliment loosened the tightness in Raphael's chest.

He dropped his head, a soft smile spreading his lips, as the clutch on his phone relaxed. Exhaling, Raphael sat down on the bed, still wet in all of his naked glory.

"Now you're just making me blush," his thick voice drummed.

Bri smiled in returned and folded her legs, intertwining them as she pulled herself back in bed to rest against her headboard.

"Now that I have to see. Raphael Valentine, blushing?"

That brought a gruff chuckle from Raphael. "If I wasn't in my own body, I don't think I would believe it either," he said. "But there's a first time for everything."

"So you're telling me you've never blushed before?"

"I can't honestly say that I have."

"Well… I just popped your cherry."

Raphael roared with laughter, and his baritone guffaw made Bri's belly flip and her pussy clench.

"It gives me pleasure to hear you laugh. You should do it more often."

Raphael's mirth subsided. "It's been a while for sure. My brothers have all tried, but it's no easy feat."

"More points for me," she teased, "soon I'll have enough to win a prize."

He chuckled again. "I love your sense of humor. I can tell you're a natural when it comes to people."

"Yeah? How so?"

"Your presence relaxes the spirit. Has anyone ever told you that?"

"No."

"But you're aware anyway, yes?"

"I am. It can be a gift or a curse." Her voice lowered. "Lately, I'm finding that it's both."

The melancholy in her voice almost crashed his heart.

"What happened?"

This time there was silence on Bri's end of the phone. She sighed. "I entrusted the financial part of my business to someone I thought had my best interest at heart, only to find out otherwise."

She shrugged. "It's a bit of a story, and since we have a breakfast meeting in a few hours, I'll wait until then to dive into the subject. Unless you need to postpone."

"No, I don't."

"Are you sure because—"

"Would it be entirely ludicrous if I said from the moment we departed I've only anticipated the instant we reunite again?"

Bri's nerves bounced, increasing her heart rate and causing a storm in her belly to kick.

"Only if that means I'm crazy for feeling the same way," she admitted.

They both lingered in separate thoughts, even though the prospect of a blooming romance mirrored them both.

"Then if it's okay with you, I'll see you at eight-thirty."

"Okay…see you then." Bri held onto the call. "Raphael, is there anything I can do to help?"

His eyes closed as the rhythm in his name rippled through his soul from the sultry tempo of her voice. There was another long silence before Raphael was able to respond with any sort of answer.

"That's very kind of you, but I'll be fine."

The silence grew again.

"All right. In that case, I'll see you in a little bit."

"*À bientôt...*" he murmured. *See you soon.*

Raphael waited for Bri to hang up, and when she did, he dropped the phone to the floor and fell back with his arms spread across his luxurious bedsheets. An exhale cruised from his lips. He must be losing his mind.

All of those years in therapy, and though he'd gotten better, never had the memory in the darkroom changed. What did that mean for him? Why was Bri there? Another drawn-out exhale shuffled from his lips.

"Bri...Bri...Bri..." he murmured.

Seconds later, Raphael lifted his head, his eyes squinting as he stared at the hard erection of his dick standing at attention. His brows furrowed deeper. "Down, boy," Raphael murmured.

He was definitely losing it.

Chapter Five

When Bri opened her front door the next morning, the delicious dream that visited her the night before was nothing compared to the man who stood in front of her.

"Good morning," his thick voice strummed.

A quirky smile manifested against her mouth. "Good morning," she responded, taking in his dark chocolate skin, gorgeous eyes, and tempting lips. Bri snagged her eye from his gaze long enough to comb them over the broad extent of his shoulders, hidden behind a thin wool blazer that opened revealing a black button-down shirt, golden cuff links, a black leather belt, and gray slacks. On his feet, black patent oxford shoes held a shine as if they'd been buffed to perfection.

Bri took a step back, feeling underdressed. Raphael's powerful gaze trailed from her soft brown orbs down a lean nose, to full lips. His stare floated over the beautiful fit of her woolen dress as it slipped over the sleek pose of her shoulders, small waist, and bodacious hips.

"Are you ready for breakfast?"

Damn right she was ready. Little did Raphael know, he was on the menu. *Don't be so thirsty.* Bri shrugged at her thought to which Raphael misinterpreted.

"You don't know if you're ready for breakfast?" he asked.

"Oh, no, I mean yes!" She sighed and calmed her nerves, inwardly urging her hormones to hush. "I am ready," she said, finally stepping toward him.

Raphael took a step back, allowing Bri to move on to the front porch. She was slightly taken aback by the not-so-chilly winds, and a frown covered her expression.

"It's not as cool as I thought it would be," she said. *As if being next to this man wouldn't make me warm enough.*

"I was surprised, too. I guess that means we'll be hot together."

Bri kept her mouth closed as her lips pursed and her cheeks crinkled from holding back a grin.

Turning to face her door, she pulled it shut and locked it quickly, then they both left her porch for the Land Rover parked in front of her building. After slipping comfortably inside, Bri adjusted herself as Raphael strolled around, got in, and easily cruised onto the road.

Bri glanced over at him, going from his tailored suit down the length of his hard body.

"Do you have plans after breakfast?" she asked.

Raphael glanced at her, then down at himself with a smirk.

"I do. Our family has partnered with the Rose family to take on the hunger crisis here in the city. Today is our first photo op for the public. It's all for show; basically to let the city know what our combined efforts are and how we plan to execute it."

Bri nodded. "That's great. I thought for a while your families didn't get along. At least that's what I heard, but I guess you have to take what you hear with a grain of salt these days."

"Actually, we were at odds for a while, but we've both found reasons to settle our dispute, and are on to bigger things."

Bri's eyes were glued to him, watching the way his arms flexed as he drove, and the easy maneuver of his cruise. The linger of his manly scent, and spicy cologne sat on the top of Bri's lip; lightly feathering her mouth but doing a number on the butterflies in her belly. Her tongue slipped to trail her lips as she fought off the wave of sudden desire that washed over her.

Raphael approached the light at Melrose, and though it was green, he paused as if considering its path.

A strong sense of anxiety fell over Bri in an instant, making her grab his hand as her expression dipped in worry on her face.

Her touch broke Raphael's pause just as a car behind them honked with an elongated shrill from the horn. Raphael glanced at her and then, deciding not to take the route, made a left turn on Meridian where he pulled into a breakfast café. The change in his aura was drastic once they'd moved past the intersection, going from anxious back to normal, and with its evolution, Bri's aura shifted as well.

"This place has good food. Have you ever eaten here?" Raphael asked. His gaze moved from the restaurant to Bri, catching the dim haze of her eyes.

"Hmm?" she said, stalled momentarily.

"I asked," his dark voice murmured, "have you ever dined here before?"

She'd re-entered the spell that bounced between them, and Raphael wasn't ignorant to the incantation.

"Oh, yes. A couple of times. They do have good food."

Raphael nodded. "Shall we?"

"Yes."

Raphael exited the car, and Bri continued to stare after him. She would bet her top dollar he had a nice ass. A giggle moved through her as Bri's mind wheeled while her gaze watched his dominant stroll to her side of the Land Rover. Opening Bri's door, Raphael offered her a hand which she accepted, slipping into his shadow, and comforted by the subtle warmth that radiated from his chest.

"Thank you."

He grinned but kept his words to himself, then with a nod eased to her right and closed the door. With his hand resting against the small of her back, they journeyed inside the restaurant and found a seat at a window that faced the downtown bustling streets.

A server approached them immediately, taking their orders then scurrying off to grab their drinks.

"A turkey sandwich on a bagel?" Bri said, smirking at Raphael's choice of food.

"I'm a brunch type of guy."

Bri laughed. "Okay, I can get that," she said with a nod.

Raphael's mouth spread into a gorgeous smile as Bri continued to chuckle.

"You find me funny?"

Bri's chuckle picked up then she swiftly slipped a hand across her mouth to calm her laughter.

"No…well, I mean, yeah. Initially, the thought of a turkey sandwich on a bagel sounds…"

"Ridiculous?"

Bri laughed again. "Hey, you said it, not me."

Raphael also snickered.

"But when you put it that way, brunch is a regular thing. I like it, too," Bri said.

"Is that why you're only eating fruit and drinking water?"

"Nope. That's so I don't pig out on our first official meeting and turn you off."

Raphael's mouth spread further as a heavy chuckle slipped from his lips. His eyes sparkled as his hearty mirth continued.

He spoke on a wave of subsiding laughter. "I rather enjoy watching your mouth move," he said.

That comment sucked the wind out of Bri, and simultaneously, their animated smiles fell as if they both caught on to the sexual implication concurrently.

"I didn't mean it like it sounded," he said.

"Yeah? How did you mean it then?" Her voice was soft

and low, sprinkled with an edge of desire that splintered through her body.

"I enjoy your company," he confessed. "Your voice," he paused, "brightens my day."

Bri's heart knocked against her breasts. "I enjoy your company as well," she admitted.

They smiled at one another, their eyes, bouncing between the slope of their noses, the edge of orchestrated eyes, and contour of their lips. Raphael cleared his throat.

"So, what happened with your photographer?"

Bri crossed her legs and rearranged her sweater, semi-thankful to be guided in the direction this breakfast was meant for. Where should she begin? Would it make sense to tell him everything or skip the specifics and head straight to the bottom line?

"Whatever you're comfortable with sharing," he said as if he could hear her thoughts or sense her trepidation.

She stared at him a moment longer. "As you are aware, Philip Daniels is my photographer. You met him at Hunter and Camilla's wedding. He owns thirty percent of Building Bridges Wedding and Event Planning. He also majored in finance, among other things, and we attended Clark Atlanta University together. To try and make a long story short, we grew close. I found a friend in him, and we agreed that he would take care of the financial part of the business. Unfortunately, I discovered yesterday that we owe some major money in taxes because he took the cash and funded his photography business."

Raphael's stare didn't reflect his thoughts. Instead, he kept a neutral gaze on her until she was finished.

"That put me in a serious bind. I have a wedding in two weeks, and that gives me no time to find a replacement. I know it's a long shot asking you, but I thought it wouldn't hurt." Her smile barely touched her lips as it dissolved before having a chance to manifest.

"Do you plan to stay in business with him?" Raphael asked.

The server approached the table with their drinks, arranging the beverages in front of them, then disappearing to get their food.

Bri took a sip of her water, then sat back against the chair.

"I don't know," she said after much thought. "Yesterday, when I found out, I was livid." She shook her head.

"But you had a chance to sleep on it," Raphael added.

Bri nodded as she held his gaze. "And that's not to say I'm okay with what he's done. I'm not. He's put the business in jeopardy. I don't know if I can trust him." Bri was sad about that, and Raphael could tell from the way her eyes trailed into the distance.

He wondered about the inner nature of Bri's and Philip's relationship. Was it merely platonic or had there ever been something more? An oddly possessive need pushed him to find out. However, in retrospect, it wasn't any of his business, so he kept the question to himself.

"What do you think I should do?"

The server resurfaced with a tray balancing in the palm of her hand.

"Excuse me," she said, crowding their space to arrange

the dishes. "Is there anything else I can get either of you at the moment?"

"I'm fine," Bri said. The server glanced at Raphael.

"Nothing for me."

"In that case, enjoy your food. I'll make my rounds to check on you in a second."

"Thank you," they said in unison.

Raphael held his hands to her, palms side up. "Should we pray over my brunch and your snack?" he teased.

Bri held on to a smirk. "Yes."

She closed her eyes, locking her fingers with the tango of his warm limbs as Raphael led them in prayer. The smooth sound of his voice invited her into the sacred place where he spoke to The Most High God. It was peaceful there, relaxing Bri right down to the bone. Every word agreed with her spirit as if they were connected somehow in that shared space, and she was almost regretful when it was over.

"In Jesus Christ's name, amen."

"Amen."

Bri exhaled a satisfying breath.

"Good?" he asked.

"Great," she said.

Raphael nodded. "I agree."

They watched each other for a long second.

"To answer your question," Raphael began, "If it were me and this is solely a business relationship, then I would not continue working with him. Here's why. Taking the money is theft. It puts your career in danger, and it sets a tone of things to look out for in the future. If you decided to stay in a working relationship, would you feel the need to constantly check behind him?"

This time, Bri exhaled, but it was heavy and loaded with distress.

"Yes, I would."

"Would that interfere with your overall process?"

"I see where you're going with this."

Raphael nodded. "There is another possible answer."

Bri leaned in, intrigued by what this other answer could entail.

"If it is a close friendship, then taking the business approach while still valid isn't the one-and-done choice to make. Friendships—real friendships that is—last a lifetime. They have to be worked on like any relationship. People make wrong decisions every day. In a friendship, you have to know when to help that person and when to cut them off.

"A business friendship may as well be a marriage because both parties are involved in a way that could crumble the empire should things go awry. The questions I asked before still remain. With you knowing the answer to them, it may be best to demote him. Take away his financial responsibility. I've heard S & M Financial Advisors downtown is a good place to start if you decide to take that route." He paused. "Or cut your losses completely."

"That would mean I'd have to buy him out," she murmured, speaking as much to Raphael as she was to herself.

"Why do I feel as if you knew that already?"

Bri sighed. "Because I did."

Raphael nodded.

"Wait, S & M Financial Advisors..." Bri tapped her chin in thought. "That's the Rose's business, right?"

"In hindsight. The wives of the Roses."

"You guys really are getting along, aren't you?"

Raphael chuckled. "I thought they were assholes. They still might be," he teased.

Bri smiled, but it didn't highlight her face, and Raphael knew it was because of her dilemma. And strangely enough, Raphael couldn't fight the intense need to want to help her rectify it.

Chapter Six

The downcast of Bri's expression sent a pang through Raphael's chest that tugged his heart.

"Don't look so sad," he said. "There's good news."

Her eyes rose to his. "Yeah?"

"Yeah," he said. "I may be able to help you out after all. At least temporarily until you figure out if you'll find a replacement."

She loved the smooth groove in his voice.

"Really?"

His smirk turned into a handsome smile, stretching the masculine edge of his mouth and kindling his face with a virile beauty.

"Sure thing, *amour.*"

When Bri first looked into the man that Raphael was, she found dozens of articles about his thriving photography business. There were pictures of him with awards and quite a few of him donating to charity.

However, there were also other photos attached to stories that spoke of the tragic accident that took his fiancée's life. Not much time after that, Raphael disappeared not only from the photography world, but he seemed to drop off the earth. No longer did he except invites to events, major or minor. For two full years, he was like a ghost, off the radar. Questions about his mental health began to circulate. It was during that second year that Raphael made his first appearance, in a live online viewing that rolled for three full minutes.

Bri was hesitant at first, unaware of what she would find behind the recording. Her inquisitiveness got the better of her, and she pressed play, choosing to hear what he had to say. She took in his chocolate face; strong, probing eyes; manly nose; and relaxed demeanor. The man was gorgeous, and he stared straight ahead for five seconds before his lips began to move.

"GOOD AFTERNOON, I AM RAPHAEL VALENTINE, AND THE purpose of this short video is to inform all who are interested that I am alive and well. I've heard your cries, and thank you for your prayers. It's taken me a while to address you because…well, because it needed to come when I was able to articulate the words.

"The last few years haven't been the easiest for me. They've been trying times and dark days. But I want to reassure you that I am not ill, and my mental state of mind is in the best hands; no need to send me any more referrals for a therapist." He chuckled. "With that being

said, the inquiries about me returning to the photography business are still not something I'm certain about. I suppose when I find the desire to shoot again, at that time, I will.

"However, I do have several portraits from my visits to New Zealand, Venezuela, Spain, Portugal, and France that will be auctioned off on a live online feed available starting this Friday, seven a.m. There will only be five of these auctions. The first showcases my shots from New Zealand.

"Again, thank you for your thoughts and prayers. Have a good day."

His voice continued to ring in her ear long after the video stopped, but Bri was stuck on his relaxed posture, firm eye contact, and the thread of his vocals that rippled through her core. He might as well have been looking right at her with the way his gaze held on to the camera. That's why asking him this question now and meeting him for breakfast didn't come with the certainty that he would acquiesce. It was a huge deal, so even though she was grateful, the last thing she wanted was to put him in a situation for which he wasn't ready.

"I never expected you to be there for me as a substitute, just for this one event. I mean, not that I don't want your help."

"It's like you said, you're in a bind and need the assistance, right?"

"Right," her voice snipped. A smile changed the direction of her mouth as she went from downcast to amazed.

He adored the way her eyes sparkled, and at the same

time, felt guilty because of it. "Then it's settled," he added, trying to shift his thoughts.

Bri lifted her fork, mindlessly tossing around the fruit in her bowl, still unsure if this was a good thing for him. "I will pay you whatever you charge." She took her eyes back up to his.

"I've got something better in mind."

Bri's brow rose. "What could be better than money for your services?"

"Run a charity race with me."

Bri paused just as she'd lifted the fork to her mouth, a dangling sliced peach ready for consumption.

"Me, a charity race?"

"Yeah, why not you?"

"You have to be in excellent shape to win one of those."

Raphael ran a keen eye over her, his gaze penetrating the woolen sweater. With a lean, his lids lowered to her thighs, and an involuntary quiver ran over Bri. Then his lids flipped up, and his tongue slid across his teeth.

"Your shape is as excellent as it gets, *amour*," he exhaled a cool breath, "if you don't mind me saying so."

His unfathomable gaze held a dark, intense magnetism that caused chills to populate in a march down her flesh.

Heat filled her cheeks, and her lashes fluttered with a bashful bat of her eyes.

"You're just saying that to be nice."

"Then that would make me a liar." He sat forward and lifted the glass in front of him to his mouth, taking a swig of the special blended natural orange juice, before coating his lips with the range of his tongue. "You don't think I would be untruthful, do you?"

Bri puckered her lips softly. "No, how could I?" She lifted a finger, pointing at him. "Unless you show me other-wise, that is."

Raphael knew she was thinking about Philip at that moment.

"Do not be discouraged," his calm voice comforted. "Not all men bear false witness. It's a child's game, and I am a man."

Another wave of warmth slipped through Bri.

Taking his turkey sandwich on a bagel in hand and a butter knife in the other, Raphael sliced the food in half. He took a piece and sat it on a napkin next to her bowl of fruit.

"What are you doing?"

"Feeding you. Besides, I know you want to try it being that you've eyed the sandwich since it arrived."

Bri giggled. *Busted again.*

"Just because the thought of a turkey sandwich on a bagel instead of bread is the most interesting choice of food I've heard thus far."

"Sweetheart, you've got to get out more."

They both laughed, soft, warm, and inviting mirth that eased their conversation even more. It left a tingle of satis-faction, that flushed over them from head to toe.

"Tell me about this charity race," Bri said, needing the reprieve.

"I thought you'd never ask." He smirked. "I've only given monetary donations before, but I'd love to do that plus a little more. The foundation is called Forget Me Not. It caters to providing support that aides victims of drunk drivers. They also educate undergraduates on the danger of getting behind the wheel inebriated. Currently, they don't offer services in Chicago, but I've watched them closely for a while and want to help them take their charity nationwide."

"Wow, that is amazing. How can I say no to that?" she teased.

Raphael smirked. "I had hoped you wouldn't."

They eyed each other silently for longer than a second.

"How many miles is the race, and when is it?"

"Two miles, one at the beginning of the course and one at the end." Bri frowned and Raphael chuckled. "It's not that type of marathon, and it's in two weeks."

"Not that type of marathon? What do you mean?"

"It's an obstacle course." Bri's eyes widened. "That sounds daunting, doesn't it?"

"You think?" Raphael's smile was wide but closed mouth.

"However, I'm always up for a challenge," Bri added.

Raphael's gaze dimmed at her preferential choice of words.

"Duly noted." Raphael took another swig of his orange juice, and Bri grabbed that opportunity to take a bite out of the turkey sandwich bagel.

"Mmmm," she moaned, consuming the food and going for a second bite.

"Good?"

Bri nodded, taking another two bites before polishing it off, then sitting against her seat.

"What is the sauce on the bagel?"

"It's a different take on honey mustard."

Bri's gaze shuffled around her, and when she found the server, she called the woman over and ordered another turkey sandwich on a bagel.

Raphael found joy in her sudden delight for his favorite brunch cuisine, and he didn't stop her when she reached across the table and lifted the remaining half.

"I'm sorry, but you should've shared a long time ago."

The beating drum of his laughter played a tune down her spine.

"To my defense, this is our first…"

She pulled her eyes from the sandwich to his piercing gaze, giving Raphael her full attention.

"Brunch with a friend," he finished.

She wondered if the thought of calling this a date bothered him. Then realized it must have since he avoided it. More importantly, Bri was dying to know what the call in the early morning was about and also his shift in demeanor at the intersection, but something told Bri he'd rather not be asked.

"You're right." She smiled. "Thank you for sharing."

He tilted his head with a nod. "Thank you for eating. I can't be walking around here with friends who starve themselves," he joked.

It was the second time he referred to her as a friend. "You consider me a friend?"

She watched his gaze drop to her lips, then back to her eyes.

"I consider you a friend, but maybe I should've asked

first." He paused. "Bri St. James, is it possible that we could be friends?"

A bashful smile eased across her lips. "I would love that," she said.

The server returned quickly with the sandwich, and in silence, they ate and lingered, neither of them wanting to depart afterward.

"Are you terribly busy today or could you spare a little more time with me?"

Bri didn't even look at her watch, nor did she check the time or care to ask.

"It looks like the rest of my day will be making phone calls to try and resolve the issues with the business. I could use a little reprieve before the headache."

"In that case, take a walk with me." Raphael pulled to his full height, his arm outstretched to take her hand.

"Sure," she said, accepting his proffered palm. Their fingers threaded on a tingling sequence of electric currents, and as they closed into one another's side, they carried their eye contact to the cash register.

He paid for brunch, and they exited the restaurant, strolling alongside one another in a lingering meander.

Do you have plans for New Year's Eve?" Raphael asked.

"I do. And I was wondering if you weren't busy if you'd like to attend a masquerade ball at the Drake Hotel."

"A masquerade ball," he said, intrigued. "That's the one hosted by the mayor of Chicago, correct?"

"Yes! You know about it?"

"I've heard a thing or two."

Bri pursed her lips. "You were invited, weren't you?"

Raphael's grin was infectious.

"Of course you were, and you probably already have a date. Am I right?"

"No," his deep voice thundered. "I haven't dated in years, nor have I desired to." He paused. "Until now." Admitting that sent another guilt-ridden wave surging over Raphael.

Being an empath, Bri could sense his apprehension. She touched his hand, the warmth of her fingers bringing his thoughts from that faraway place to the safety of her face. Again, she wanted to go into detail about last night, and though she'd done her research, she needed to hear from him how he was dealing with his late-fiancée's death.

"You can talk to me about it," she said.

They paused their stroll, and a shuffling current of wind sailed around them from the velocity of neighboring traffic.

Raphael squeezed her hand in reassurance. "I'm okay. As for the masquerade ball," he said, changing the subject, "I appreciate the invite, but I'm old-school *amour*."

Bri's brows furrowed. "What does that mean?"

"Never would I allow a friend to beat me to the punch in asking for a date." He steadied the thump behind the muscular wall of his chest, then licked his lips and went with his heart. "But it would be my pleasure if you could be my plus one."

Bri's heart ricocheted as her thoughts tumbled. A coy smile quirked at the side of her mouth, and she warmed as her pulse fluttered.

"Tell me right now if that's going to be a problem," he added.

Bri pursed her lips and folded her arms. "What if it is?" she teased. "I am an independent woman, you know."

He nodded. "This, I am aware, but I'm not a fifty-fifty type of man, *amour*. I'll wrestle you about it if I need to."

Another splintering wave of heat covered her, and her mouth spread into a daring smile. "I was only kidding," she said.

"Good," his easy voice drummed. "Then we have an understanding?"

Bri nodded. "So bossy," she teased.

"You think so? It's not my intention to be."

"I know, that's what makes you all the more attractive."

Raphael's brow quirked along with the corner of his mouth. "You find me attractive?"

Bri giggled, feeling bubbly like a teenager. She couldn't remember the last time she felt so carefree and light on her feet. Her hand fell from his, and she stepped ahead, turning to face him as her feet lightly backpedaled.

"You know you're a handsome man."

A laugh came from him. "You're deflecting…"

"I'm not!" she protested with a lift of her finger.

His gaze dropped, and he twisted his lips, making a tumbling laugh bellow from Bri's mouth.

"What?" she said, excitedly holding her arms out. She tried to hold on to another abounding laugh, but it escaped her as she twirled to hide her face. The shift in her movement was quick and unsteady, making her accidentally step from the sidewalk into the street.

A blaring horn from a racing sedan pierced the air as it headed straight for Bri. Raphael's heart dropped, and in a flash, he was transported back to that fateful day four years prior.

He didn't stay there for long; a split second later, his legs moved, arms shot out, and massive hands gripped Bri with sudden agility. He snatched her from the street just as the car flew past them, then turned his back to the haste of wind and traffic while burying her in the immense width of his chest.

His broad shoulders rose and fell along with his unsteady breaths. With his eyes closed and his forehead buried into hers, he murmured, "Please…" his dark voice simmered against her face. "Stay…"

Bri was shaken to her core, her eyes wide and heart pounding recklessly at his plea.

Raphael reiterated, "Stay on the right side of me. Okay?" His breathing was a continued labor of unease, his body tense, his jaw half-locked.

Bri nodded like a bobblehead. "I'm—" she stuttered. "I'm sorry." Her hands slipped up his shoulders to his neck, then his face where her palms settled against the warm, rugged cut of his jaw. "I wasn't paying attention, I…"

Raphael nodded, his eyes still closed as he worked to calm his racing heart. When his gaze flipped to hers, Bri was crushed by the fear that rested there and the overcast of moisture that tried to hide behind his lids. Her throat clogged as a knot formed behind her esophagus.

"Raphael…"

He didn't respond, only held on to her for dear life with no other words gravitating between them for minutes on end. She felt him tremble mildly against her body, realizing the type of distress that rested on his shoulders even for a brief second. They held on to one another, breaths tingling, pulses thumping, and mouths hovering, Raphael's over Bri's.

When he finally calmed his nerve, Raphael's thick voice stroked her flesh. "Are you all right?"

"Yes," she responded quickly. "Are you?"

They eyed one another, and Raphael blinked back the fear as if putting it behind a locked door. His gaze was heavy but reassuring as he nodded.

"Maybe we should go back inside."

Raphael released the tight hold he had on her and slowly checked his Rolex.

"I need to head to this photo op." His voice had gone back to its normal tone, but Bri could still sense his stress. "Let me get you back home."

Bri sighed. "Okay."

Raphael reassured Bri he was fine, but when one strong hand grabbed hers, Raphael's fingers linked tightly, and he didn't let go until she was safely back in her studio apartment.

Chapter Seven

$\mathcal{B}$ri forced herself to keep up with the incline of the treadmill. As her legs ran in steady marches, a line of sweat dripped from the edge of her hairline. Her thoughts remained heavy on Raphael. Not hearing from him in the past two days made her wonder if she should be worried. And here lately, she was leaning toward concern.

On a machine next to her, Mrs. St. James kept up with her daughter's strides while keeping an invested eye on Bri. Something about her focus was off, but Mrs. St. James couldn't put her finger on it.

"Two minutes," Mrs. St. James shouted.

That seemed to make Bri pick up speed as if she were racing to cross an invisible finish line. Her thighs burned as the treadmill rose, making the incline more difficult.

"Sixty seconds," Mrs. St. James called.

Simultaneously, they ran, as if something behind them

would devour their existence if they didn't make it to their destination.

"Thirty seconds!"

Bri's heart clamored behind her breasts, and instead of breathing through her nose, she sprinted the last thirty seconds with her mouth parted and her eyes straightforward.

"Ten, nine, eight, seven…"

Suddenly, blinded by droplets of perspiration, Bri closed her eyes but kept her legs moving.

"Bring it down a notch!" Mrs. St. James called.

Bri tried to follow her mother's instructions, but her adrenaline was high, and her thoughts drifted from their current place.

"Are you all right?"

She heard Raphael's voice.

"Yes," she responded quickly. "Are you?"

Fear rested in his gaze as he nodded.

"Brittney St. James!"

Bri snapped from her reverie to her mother's face, her legs still moving even after their time had expired.

"Bring it down, Brittney and cut your machine off!"

Bri punched a few buttons, and her gallop dwindled as her legs slowed to a jog before finally stopping. She stepped off the machine, then bent over, dropping her arms against her thighs and holding there as she reined in her breath.

"Not so fast, get your breathing under control," Mrs. St. James said.

Bri nodded and regained control of her breath.

"That's good." Mrs. St. James rubbed her daughter's back while watching Bri in the same bent-over position.

Bri nodded again and glanced at her mother, reassuring her that she was under control.

"Okay," Mrs. St. James said. She left Bri's side to stroll to a refrigerator posted in the corner of the equipment room. After removing a bottle of water, she made her way back to Bri and handed it over.

"Thanks."

Bri twisted the cap then stood and tossed the water back. She drank thirstily, then took a few more calming breaths before eyeing her mom.

"What's going on with you?" Mrs. St. James asked.

"What do you mean?"

"Are you really going to stand there and act as if nothing happened just now?"

"What happened?"

Mrs. St. James was a mirror image of Bri; same soft brown eyes, coffee-brown skin, and shoulder-length hair. They stood eye to eye, both five feet six inches off the ground and fit with curvy hips that were generational.

Mrs. St. James sank her hands into her waist and peered at her daughter.

"Our time ran out, but you kept running almost like you weren't here. Where'd you go?"

Bri's thoughts shifted back to Raphael.

"There," Mrs. St. James said. "Where are you now?"

Bri blinked back to focus on her mother's face, but before she could say anything, Mrs. St. James went further.

"Does this have anything to do with the new guy you're dating?"

Bri frowned. "What are you talking about? I'm not dating any guy."

"For a minute, I thought you were just waiting to tell me, but you actually look genuinely confused." Mrs. St. James strolled to the entrance and lifted a newspaper that sat on a nearby table. She held it up. "*This* guy."

Bri crossed the room in a quick trot, taking the paper out of her mother's hands. Her eyes bulged when they scurried across the headline.

"In a rare photo, world-renowned photographer Raphael Valentine was spotted outside of a breakfast café on the corner of Meridian and Ninth Street comforting Bri St. James, an award-winning wedding planner who just so happened to be the bridal coordinator for Raphael's brothers, Lance and Hunter Valentine. Patrons inside the café said the two enjoyed an early breakfast and fed one another as they indulged in conversation. Our team reached out to Raphael for comment but have yet to receive a response.

Could there be a love connection brewing?

A picture of Bri clutched in Raphael's arms, with his forehead resting against hers was prominent across the page.

Heat stung her cheeks. "Oh my God." She was shocked into momentary silence as her mind reeled from what she read and saw. Bri's eyes shifted to the date in the right-hand corner of the newspaper. "This was yesterday's paper." Her eyes flipped to her mother's. "How did I miss this?"

"I certainly don't know. It's *only* been news for the last couple of days."

"Are you kidding me?" Bri was devastated. What if this was the reason Raphael hadn't reached out? Maybe he didn't want people to get the wrong idea.

"What's going on, baby girl?"

Bri sighed and turned away from her mother, slowly treading back to stand in front of the treadmill.

"It all started when I was planning Hunter and Camilla Valentine's wedding."

Bri went into detail. She and her mother were close, always had been, so talking like best friends was their thing. For Bri, it felt good to confide in her mother; sharing their life experiences became their favorite pastime. By the time she brought her mother up to speed, Bri's mind was already moving back to Raphael and his well-being.

"It sounds like you two are in-like with each other."

Bri shut her eyes and let go of a weary breath. "What am I supposed to do about that?" Bri murmured.

"The question is, what do you want to do about it?"

Bri took a sip of her water as her eyes scurried around the wall of the room. "I'm not sure if he's...ready. You know."

Mrs. St. James moved to stand in front of her daughter.

"I don't know, but I understand. I don't have the answer that you're looking for. The most I could offer is follow your heart and make sure that your mind aligns."

Mrs. St. James laid a soft hand on her daughter's shoulder, and Bri shook from her thoughts to glance at her mom.

"You know you always have good ideas. Even when you don't have any advice, it's good."

They laughed softly, and Mrs. St. James nodded. "Let me fix us some lunch."

"I'm down."

The duo pivoted, then left the room, Mrs. St. James with thoughts of mini chicken salad sandwiches on the brain and Bri only entertaining thoughts of Raphael.

Chicago Waldorf Astoria
Penthouse Suite

THE INK PEN RESTING BETWEEN RAPHAEL'S FINGERS HOVERED idly just above the blank sheet of his notebook. Writing had always been his reprieve, allowing his muse to carry burdens to the page and create words that released his silent thoughts, often helped Raphael restore balance within himself.

At first, those words were incensed, unstable, and full of anguish. But after many years of therapy, they became more solid, focused, and transparent. That was until two days ago when his spirit had been rocked by the sudden dread of Bri St. James being run over by morning traffic.

His hand remained suspended as his mind rotated around the incident, entertaining the panic that settled in his gut all over again.

Raphael exhaled a deep breath and dropped the pen on the journal. He sat in quiet solitude, brimming with a tsunami of thoughts that argued back and forth like two separate entities.

When this happened in the beginning, Raphael would sometimes be stuck in a storm of heartrending musings. But after seeing Dr. Mark Fortner, his therapist for the last four years, Raphael could now distinguish the truth between thé noise.

From the day his life changed on that fateful afternoon, Raphael was sure his era of loving someone had come and gone. At the time, his mind couldn't contemplate other blissful moments like those he shared with Chastity. But oddly, the unexpected flood of emotions that flocked to his heart when around Bri St. James made him reconnect with a tenderness that questioned the inevitability he once under-stood to be true.

On autopilot, Raphael rose to his feet and left his home studio room, venturing down an extended hallway to enter the kitchen. The abundance of natural light that poured through the twelve-foot ceiling windows lit up the spacious interior, casting rays of sunlight across stainless steel appliances and marble countertops.

There, he turned on the stove to make a pot of coffee, old-school style, and while he waited, headed for the outdoor terrace to take in a breath of fresh air. Overlooking the city, the fifty-eighth-floor penthouse suite had a magnifi-cent view that seemed to stretch with the order of clouds that tap-danced along the light blue sky.

Inhaling a deep breath, Raphael shook the morning's stormy thoughts, clearing his mind and choosing to free himself from its clutches. In a pair of blue jean and a casual button-down shirt, Raphael approached the railing and perched the palms of his outstretched hands against the cool metal. Raphael's shirt was unbuttoned, revealing the solidity of his muscular torso, and the stone ground beneath his feet was cool as a gust of wind sailed between his toes.

The chime of his ringing doorbell sounded to the reaches of his opened terrace door. He checked his wrist-watch, knowing if someone was at his door they had access to his floor, which he only reserved for family.

He left the balcony for the front door and without demanding the visitor announce themselves, opened the entrance to see who was on the other side.

"Dre," his said, opening the door wider to allow his brother entrance.

DeAndre Valentine moved across the threshold, closing the access behind him, then following Raphael into the kitchen.

"To what do I owe this visit? Did you land the NASA deal?"

DeAndre Valentine was the mastermind behind Valentine Innova-Corp, a civil engineering company that, within the last quarter of the year, had also taken on aerospace engineering.

"Not yet, brother. We're still in negotiations."

"Coffee?"

"Yeah."

DeAndre strolled to the island, his presence adding an extra layer of testosterone to the room. He stood the same height as Raphael with smooth chocolate skin that was accentuated on his heavy build.

"How are you holding up?" DeAndre asked.

Raphael lifted the pot from the stove and poured two mugs of steaming coffee, then added a scoop of sugar to each before stirring and passing one to his brother.

"I've had my days, but for the most part, I'm good, and getting better every day, I think."

"You think?" DeAndre blew across the surface of the steaming mug.

Raphael sucked his teeth. "Okay, so for the last four years, I've been okay with being alone. You know I've only been invested in recovering from Chastity's death and finding ways to make the community aware of the dangers of drinking and driving."

DeAndre nodded as Raphael sat his mug down, then folded his arms.

"But lately..." he paused.

DeAndre observed him with a piercing eye.

"I don't know."

"You don't know if you want to be alone or am I missing something?"

"The thing is, it's not about being with someone again. It's about a specific someone."

A singular brow rose on DeAndre's face. "Do I know this someone?"

"In a way."

"Does someone have a name?"

Raphael smirked and nodded slowly. "Bri St. James."

A smile registered across DeAndre's mouth. "I knew the moment you kissed her at Lance's wedding."

Raphael tilted his head to side-eye his brother. "How could you tell?"

DeAndre sat his mug down. "You haven't looked at another woman since Chastity. That was my first clue. But to pull her in the way you did…" DeAndre shook his head once. "I knew she must've penetrated your heart in some way to do that. What I want to know is how did I miss it?"

"The same way I did," Raphael responded. "I couldn't comprehend what I felt until we were in that moment." DeAndre eyed him skeptically. "I mean that. Her personality rubbed off on me, and I don't know how it attached itself. I was blinded by the flowers at Hunter's wedding when I noticed her. The energy between us is…"

DeAndre leaned in, waiting to hear the words slip from Raphael's mouth.

"Undeniably intoxicating. I feel pulled to her as if she is the reason I'm still here." Raphael's faraway gaze slipped back to DeAndre's face. "Is that asinine?"

DeAndre lifted the mug and mused on his brother's words. "Not at all, brother. Only the man upstairs knows why the chess pieces fall into place like they do. My question to you is, how do you feel about that?"

Raphael mused as he took a sip of his coffee. "I'm not sure. On the one hand, I need to explore it; so much so that she asked me for a favor, and I complied even after I slept on it and told myself I couldn't do it."

DeAndre sat the mug back down. "What favor?"

Raphael went over his and Bri's morning conversation while DeAndre hung on every word as if it was religious scripture.

"You're going to be her photographer?"

Raphael nodded.

"In the public eye, on a regular basis?"

Raphael nodded again. He, too, couldn't believe what he'd agreed to.

"Okay," DeAndre said. "This is progress. Good progress," he added. "Right?"

Raphael held his mug to his lips in thought.

"Do you think it's a mistake?" DeAndre asked.

"No."

That answer came quickly, DeAndre thought.

"Okay then. Does she know about——"

"I believe so."

"But you haven't told her yourself?"

"No." Raphael eyed his brother. "You think I should?"

"It's up to you. Do you think you two will get serious?"

"Whoa." Raphael held a hand out. "You do know what you're asking me?"

"I do." DeAndre thought it over more. "It's too soon," he determined.

"I like her," Raphael admitted. His gaze fell from DeAndre's, and he spoke with his mind in a fog. "I adore her." His gaze rejoined DeAndre's. "But I don't know if I can forgive myself long enough for it to turn into anything else."

"Forgive yourself?"

"It should've been me."

DeAndre placed the mug on the counter. "I was under the assumption that you understood you weren't responsible for Chastity's——"

"I do understand that. Doesn't mean it should've been her."

The two men watched each other for a drawn-out spell.

"Are you still seeing Dr. Fortner?"

"Once a month."

DeAndre nodded, and another long thread of silence lapsed between them before DeAndre spoke.

"Brother, Chastity was a great woman, and I know she wouldn't want you to torture yourself forever. Don't you know she would be happy for you?"

Raphael didn't respond, only stared at his brother before lifting his mug and turning his back to empty it and pour a fresh cup.

"We can be friends," Raphael said, his back still turned. He spoke as if it was his final say on the matter.

"You don't have to make a decision now. Who knows if Bri is meant to be a friend or someone more? For now, enjoy her company, and everything else will fall into place."

Raphael turned around and leaned his taut derriere against the countertop. He nodded and took a sip, knowing he hadn't revealed the emotions that he'd tangled with over the last forty-eight hours. Neither had he informed his brother of the dream or the encounter in front of the café. For Raphael, he was still breaking down what it all meant. Why did he miss talking to her as if they were long-lost friends?

"What are your plans for New Year's Eve?" DeAndre asked, pulling Raphael from his muse but shifting his thoughts right back to Bri.

"Mayor Luke Steele is hosting the masquerade ball at The Drake Hotel."

"Wait, you're going out?"

Raphael smirked. "What did you think I was going to say, I'm sitting at home with a bottle of brandy watching the sky light up alone?"

DeAndre's eyes shifted side to side, "Yeah, something like that."

The two men guffawed.

"Not this year."

DeAndre nodded. "I think I like this new Raphael that's coming out. Could Bri St. James be the reason for your sudden boldness?"

Raphael tried to hide a smile behind the steaming cup of coffee.

"What the hell, brother, are you blushing?" DeAndre couldn't believe his eyes. "Get the…" DeAndre waved him off and a full-on guffaw roared from Raphael.

The laugh felt good to his soul, and Raphael cuddled his chest as the mirth slipped from his lips. "I'd flip you off," Raphael said, "but it's not my style."

DeAndre laughed heartily. "Are you going alone?"

There was a long pause before Raphael opened his mouth to answer.

"Wait, don't tell me. Bri is going with you?"

"Are you asking me?"

"That's a yes," DeAndre said, answering his own question.

"I didn't say that."

"Yes, you did." DeAndre felt good about this date, and

now he wanted to see it play out for himself. "I can tag along if you want me to."

"Why, because I need my little brother's shoulder to lean on?" Raphael joked.

Born septuplets to media moguls Leslie and Bridgette Valentine, Raphael and his brothers were continually holding their title of big brother over the next sibling under them.

"Two minutes, you hold that title by two minutes," DeAndre said.

Raphael barked out a laugh, his legs taking off into a swaggered stroll. "I need to make a phone call; I hope you don't mind." He continued down the corridor, headed back to his home studio where he'd left his cell.

Inside, Raphael turned the phone over in his palm. He was on the cusp of a new year, which could mean new beginnings, new opportunities, new...love, perhaps? He sighed and tapped the phone against his forehead then swiftly dialed her number without giving it a second, third, or fourth thought.

Chapter Eight

The Drake Hotel
10:45 P.M.
New Year's Eve

*O*f all nights to be running late... Bri St. James shuffled to the awaiting limo and eased inside as the chauffeur closed the door. At the last minute, the boutique she ordered her dress from months in advance called to inform her that the carrier still hadn't delivered her custom order.

"Why am I just now getting a phone call? I need this dress tonight," she huffed, twirling on her heels and plopping down in her office chair.

"I'm sorry, Ms. St. James, we take full responsibility for this mix-up."

"Well, what are you going to do about it?"

The woman on the other end covered the phone with a hand and spoke to someone in the background. Bri tried to listen in on her muffled conversation, but it was no use.

"Ms. St. James," the woman said, coming back to the phone.

"Yes."

"We have a collection of limited-edition gowns here in the store. You're more than welcome to come down and pick one for your evening, and we'll refund fifty percent of your custom order."

Bri sighed. "I'll be down in an hour."

She hung up the phone and prayed on her way to the boutique that this "collection" would hold up to the dress she initially wanted to wear. While she sprinted across town, Bri texted Raphael to let him know she wouldn't be ready in time. Hearing from him after days of silence was refreshing and pulled her from a funk she wasn't aware she was harboring. Since then, text messages between the two had come regularly, and Bri was hoping to keep it that way.

I'm sorry, there was a mix up with my gown, I'm going to be late.

She sent the message, and minutes later received an answer.

I'll wait for you.

A rising tide of warmth filled her completely.

You can't be late. You're the Mayor's guest.

Send.

I'm only attending to be there with you, *Amour*.

A vibrating tingle ran down her skin, and Bri's heart

palpitated behind her breasts. As much as it pleased her, Bri didn't want Raphael to be late because of her.

Let's make a deal. You'll arrive on time, and I'll show up fashionably late, how's that?

She sent a smiling face emoji with the message as a tickle ran through her. Seconds later, another incoming notification arrived.

You drive a hard bargain. But I'm willing to meet you halfway. I'll arrive on time, but I'm also sending a limo to pick you up. Regardless of how late you are, my chauffeur will wait until you're ready.

Bri blushed and texted back.

Deal.

NOW IN THE BACKSEAT OF THE LIMO, BRI HAD A NOTION TO look over herself again although she'd done it a thousand times already. Her hair was pinned to the top of her head, showing off her swan-like neck that was covered in chocolate coated skin. Black bejeweled earrings hung from her ears like crystals, and a royal blue mask covered her eyes, resting just above Bri's high cheekbones. From there, the disguise rose high above her head and spread into black feathers like that of a peacock.

The dress was royal blue and covered in shiny blue tassels. It shimmered off her curvaceous figure, carrying a split up the middle of her right thigh, revealing smooth bare legs. Tonight, Bri decided to leave the pantyhose behind. She felt daring and spicy in the gown alone, and she was secretly hoping that Raphael would find her appearance sexy and not scandalous. Bringing in the New Year with Raphael excited Bri, and she wanted to share that intimate moment with him even after the midnight hour.

Butterflies rummaged in her stomach as the limo navigated toward Michigan Avenue to pull in front of The Drake Hotel. Bri took in the scenery around them; luxury vehicles were jam-packed, causing traffic to gridlock.

"Whew...here we go," she whispered to herself. She waited in the backseat while they navigated to the entrance and parked.

The chauffeur waited for another spell, and Bri wondered why he made no move to open her door. She shrugged, then reached for the handle to do it herself when it opened, and the palm of an outstretched masculine hand reached inside offering help.

"Oh!" Bri covered her chest. "Raphael, you scared me."

The kick in her heartbeat settled.

"Forgive me, *amour*; I didn't mean to startle you."

Bri accepted his hand, and together, they moved beyond the interior of the limo where Bri was pulled into the breadth of his chest.

It was then that she took in his attire, dapper in a black tailored suit jacket, dark button-down Tom Ford shirt, and black pants that complemented the multilayered edges of his rigid physique. Behind a royal blue and black mask, half of Raphael's face was enclosed while the other half was exposed. His forehead, nose, and hard cheekbones remained hidden, but the lush succulence of his lips and groomed beard were unmistakably eye-catching. He was wickedly handsome, and Bri had a notion to move into his mouth for a taste of his lips, but she remained poised, waiting for his order.

"*Vous êtes belle*," he murmured.

Bri smirked and slowly translated his words inwardly. *You are beautiful.* She watched as the outline of his blue gaze traveled over every inch of her form, pausing in places that made her shiver and stepped into the prominence of his physique.

"*Merci*," she responded in thanks, her voice a husky strum of allure. "How did you know I was out here?"

Raphael moved to her side and held his arm up where Bri intertwined her limb with his. Together, they started a slow stroll down the red carpet.

"I've been waiting for you, remember?"

"Yes, I do."

They smiled at the flashes of cameras and made their entrance without being stopped.

"Thank you."

Raphael glanced down at her. "For?"

"Waiting. Most men would've made me come in and hunt them down."

She laughed lightheartedly, but Raphael paused their stroll and turned to face her. "Then most men are idiots, and they do not deserve to be in the presence of a queen."

His intense gaze ransacked her nerves, spiraling a rain of shivers down her body. "You're sweet," she said, holding his eye. "The sweetest I've ever known."

Raphael exhaled deeply. His attraction to her became more evident by each passing second. Even over the days they went without communication, Raphael could feel her growing on him. From the moment they'd met, her sincerity for his well-being as a stranger was heartwarming, and seeing Bri put in work around the clock reminded him of the drive needed to become successful at any endeavor. Raphael lifted her hand to his mouth, placing a warm kiss, a firm and indulgent mixture, in a brand against her skin.

He felt her quiver as he interlocked her fingers with his. "Dance with me."

A smile curved at the corners of her lips. "Lead the way."

They moved in sync, meandering through the sea of masks as people danced around each other, drinking and indulging in merriment conversation. As they made it to the middle of the floor, the song hailing through the surround sound changed, and the smooth vocalist H.E.R. began to serenade the room with her hit, "Best Part," featuring Daniel Caesar.

Raphael's arm slipped around Bri's waist where he pulled her close, keeping her eye contact. With his other hand linked with hers, they swayed to the strum of a guitar as the songstress crooned about being held close and kissed slowly.

Bri inhaled and exhaled, her breasts rising and falling against the hard plank of his washboard abdomen. Like a skilled dancer, Raphael's waltz was smooth in transition, twirling her in a way that she could keep up without wondering what the next steps were. Their heartbeats matched as a thrill of desire poured over them, through and through. When Daniel Caesar began to sing, Bri couldn't help but align his lyrics with the thoughts of Raphael. She wondered if he saw the sunrise in her brown eyes like the neo-soul singer so elegantly sang about. Or if she should get outside of her head and realize it's just a record and nothing more. With that last thought, Bri's eyes dropped from his magnificent gaze and quickly scurried across the décor of the room in an effort to shake her contemplation.

Royal blue drapery hung from the walls with a mixture of black and crystal chandeliers that suspended from the ceiling. Next to them, trapped in a net hanging in decorative patches, were bundles of balloons that Bri assumed would be released at the stroke of midnight.

"I thought your dress didn't come in time," Raphael said, his gruff undertone ravishing her body in chills.

Bri brought her eye back to him then took a meager step back and glanced over herself. "It didn't." She smiled up at him. "But thankfully, they had something that worked in its place."

Raphael's thick brow arched. "So you're saying the custom gown you were fitted for is more dangerous than this?"

Bri giggled. "Dangerous?"

"You don't know how absolutely stunning you are, do you?"

Her heart lurched, and her pussy thumped, taking her by surprise. She almost squealed from the heated pull between her thighs, and on instinct, she crushed them together in an attempt to calm her vagina down.

"Um, thank you." Her voice was a shaken whisper. She cleared it quickly. "I was hoping you would approve."

Raphael's body temperature was past smoking. There was a never-ending fever that scorched him.

"Were you?"

She blushed. "Yeah."

Raphael leaned closer to her as if telling a secret only she should hear. "I would approve if you were in a brown paper bag, *amour*."

Bri laughed, opening her mouth. The spread of her lips displayed pearly white teeth that lifted the sparkle in her eyes and increased the rapturous beat in his chest.

"You did not just say a brown paper bag!"

Her enjoyment stirred his gut, and the vibration of her body against his as she laughed hardened the lowest region of him. He took a purposeful step back in order not to alarm her. But she assumed it was a simple groove in his step and instinctively, she closed the gap with a twist of her hips to the music.

It was the first brush that brought her attention to the solid length of his erection, and the rippling contact coaxed a drip from her pussy.

"Oh…"

It came out like a moan and apology in the same breath.

"Forgive me," he said. "This has never happened before." He was half embarrassed, but it was becoming more difficult to control his libido around her.

Bri was in the same boat, Raphael was just none the wiser. He took another step backward, and again, Bri followed him, refusing to break their connection.

"*Amour…*"

It was a warning, one that Bri St. James was hell-bent on ignoring.

"I don't mind it, Raphael."

They eyed each other in a piercing battle that spun them from the room and cloaked them in their own universe.

"I don't think you understand."

"Look, Raphael, I…like you, in a way that extends past a mere friendship. I hope you don't mind me saying so."

His pulse thumped with an extra layer of vigor as she went on.

"I'm glad you called the other day. I was worried after I didn't hear from you."

His face softened while holding on to its masculinity. "I apologize. My silence was because of me, not you. It's been my way of providing cover for myself since…" His words tapered off, and Raphael redirected his speech. "I want to be open with you, *amour*. When we're together, there's this natural flow between us that I can't quite gather. I see you in 3-D. Everything around you is alive, and your spirit seems to interlace with mine. Even hearing your voice rings on a different frequency. I can't explain it, but it's refreshing like nothing I've experienced before." He took a deep breath, and Bri's heart throbbed as he spoke his truth.

"When you stepped in the street…" he pulled in a slow dragging breath and Bri waited, breathless for him to continue, "I had to wonder if maybe I was bad luck for you."

Bri's mouth parted, a gasp slipping from her lips as her heart continued its racket. "Oh no…" She reached out and touched his face, her palm soothing against the rough terrain of his beard. She shook her head. "Don't ever think that. If anything, I am lucky to have met you. A man who puts others before himself is a blessing. Never a curse. You didn't have to invest time or money into Forget Me Not charity, you didn't have to attend your brother's weddings after what happened to you, and they wouldn't have minded. Nor did you have to put yourself in a position to help me when being in public is not your thing." She shook her head again. "And look at you now. I think this is a record. You, in public, among partygoers." She smiled, and Raphael grinned.

"That's because of you," he said. "I wanna be where you are..."

The heat around them swallowed the two in a cocoon that tinged their skin. Their gazes bounced off of one another, and Raphael released her hand to cover Bri's waist in a gripping hold that flushed her breasts in a hot graze against his chest.

Bri's heart fluttered. "I feel the same way."

Their pulses thumped, libidos rising as they floated closer, seconds from capturing one another's lips.

A loud squeal resounded from a microphone, and a voice boomed out of the loudspeaker. "Testing, one, two." A few snickers floated about. "I'm going to make this brief," the mayor said.

Raphael and Bri paused their drift, hanging in suspension as the voice drew their attention.

"I want to take a moment and thank you, Chicago, for coming to bring in the new year with my lovely fiancée and me." Mayor Luke Steele carried his gaze over to Jasmine

Alexandria Rose. She smiled, fixated on him like he was the only man in the room. Mayor Steele kissed her lips, receiving shouts and catcalls from the audience. Others laughed, while men whistled, and some stomped the grounds.

Mayor Steele guffawed, winked, then continued. "We have forty minutes until the new year!"

The building shook as the crowd erupted in cheers, some holding glasses of bubbly while others knocked hips in salutations.

A server paused in front of Raphael and Bri, and Raphael looked down at her.

"Would you like something to drink?"

"I would."

Raphael removed two flutes from the tray and thanked the server. He passed Bri the tumbler, and she took a hefty sip, drinking the spirit halfway. They returned their attention to the mayor.

"In ten minutes, we'll start a roundabout shuffle. When the music starts, you dance. When it stops, you change partners and keep up your flow. Now, fellas if you're married or engaged, make sure not to go too far. You would probably fare well to dance on the side of your sister."

The room lit up in laughter again, and Jasmine could be seen shaking her head. "We'll dance until the countdown starts, five minutes before midnight."

"Wooo!" somebody shouted from the crowd. Another round of laughter bounced throughout the room.

"Precisely!" Mayor Steele agreed. "But here's the most

important part. Drink responsibly, call a car service, a friend or…" He held his arms out. "Get a room!"

The crowd shouted with howls from the men and purrs from the women. "We are, after all, at the Drake Hotel, and to show I mean business, there's a block of rooms on hold for anyone who may need one."

The building shook again as the crowd erupted once more. Mayor Steele held his arm up to calm the audience.

"As a disclaimer, I'd like to point out the mayor's office doesn't condone any behavior that may come out of staying in one of these rooms. They are merely to keep you from behind the wheel in the event that you've been drinking."

"And we appreciate you, mayor!" another guy shouted.

More cheers, screams, and laughter ensued. Mayor Steele couldn't contain his guffaw as he bent his head in amusement. "With that being said, enjoy your night and get ready to waltz!"

More stomps, claps, and shouts rang out as the mayor passed the microphone to his left, and music seeped back through the speakers.

Bri downed the rest of her champagne as she and Raphael locked eyes again.

"The mayor just reminded me." Raphael reached inside his pocket and pulled a key from inside. "I hope you don't mind, but I took the necessary precaution and booked you a room. You're on the top floor with a code so only you can gain access to the floor."

"Raphael, you didn't have to do that."

"I'm looking out for you, so let me do it, woman."

Bri's tongue teased the corner of her mouth, smitten

with his charm. "Does that mean you'll be staying here, too?"

"I will," his husky voice strummed.

"Mmm, so you also have a room, or are we staying together?"

Raphael's lids lowered to her mouth. "I have a room." He spoke again as his gaze met hers, "I wouldn't be presumptuous enough to assume you would be okay staying in close quarters with me. But why do I feel like you are aware of this?"

Music floated through the speakers, and the crowd grew close for the beginning of the waltz.

"Because I am."

"Hmm…"

Raphael closed in, discarding her flute to a nearby waiting tray held up by a server standing idly by.

One of his arms slipped around her while the other found her hand to begin their step dance.

"I don't know how to waltz," Bri admitted.

"I'll lead the way."

Her hips swayed with his steps—two steps forward, two side to side, then two steps back. Bri couldn't stop the gyrating in her swing, adding flavor to the dance that spiced up their moves and drove their loins insane.

With a hand pressed gently at the small of her back, Raphael paused, then rocked, and with a twist, dipped her, stretching Bri's curvaceous frame and reveling in the showcase of her extended neck. It was no use fighting off the sting of desire that filled him. It was a losing battle that

Raphael was prepared to surrender to. Had it not been for his clear rationale, maybe he would've.

Bri rose up slowly, guided by the pull of his strong hands. The music faded then stopped, and on a twirl, it started back up again as Bri was handed off to a nearby partygoer. The transition came with ease, but the difference in the change of energy was instant, and Bri's yearning to reconnect with Raphael's aura caused her eyes to follow him around the ballroom.

She was handed off again, and on the fourth exchange, her vision was cut from Raphael's entirely. Blinking from a haze, Bri looked into the eyes of her partner and noticeably felt his smile was familiar.

"I didn't know you could waltz," he said.

Bri's partial smile faded. "Philip?" She blinked back a frown as Philip led their dance.

"For a second, I didn't think you would notice me," he said.

Confused, Bri let out a frustrated sigh. "What are you doing here?"

"It's New Year's Eve, and I figured you would be here. I've been trying to reach you all week, but you've been avoiding me."

He turned, and she stepped in line, not wanting to break the groove of partygoers nearby.

"And for good reason," she hissed.

"I'm sorry," he apologized.

"Good, now that we've got that out of the way, you can leave."

"Bri, I mean it."

"I do, too, and this is not the time for this conversation."

"Well, when is? You won't return my calls or emails. How am I supposed to get through to you?"

"You're not!" she snapped. "When I'm ready to talk, I'll get in touch with you."

She shimmied out of his grasp and turned to walk away, but he stepped forward and cut her off. "Bri, please don't do this. We've been friends forever. I can't lose you now."

"Seriously, Philip, some friend you are."

She pushed past him again, but he gripped her arm.

"Let me go." She tried to shake out of his grasp, but he tightened it.

"Bri, listen to me."

"Let me go!" His grip was like a vise. "What the hell is wrong with you?"

Philip didn't get a chance to respond before the growl of an ominous voice severed their confrontation.

"Have you lost…your fuckin' mind?"

Raphael didn't wait for an answer; on instinct, his massive palm gripped Philip's neck and squeezed his esophagus, releasing Bri from Philip's snare.

Bri's eyes grew wide. "Raphael!" His gaze shot daggers at Philip, who struggled to breathe and grappled at Raphael's hands to be released.

"Please," she said. "Look at me." Her hand slipped up his face. "Baby…"

Raphael's dark gaze shifted to Bri's. She smiled slightly. "We're growing an audience."

His stare was sturdy, and with another tight crush of his fingers, Raphael tossed Philip back, releasing him with a shove. The few eyes that turned their way took in the scene with mystery, but because of the masks, no one but the three involved knew who or what the incident was about.

When Philip caught his breath, he glared at Raphael and went to speak.

"Leave," was all Raphael said. He wouldn't say more, and Philip thought better of stepping up to antagonize him. Instead, Philip glanced between Raphael and Bri, questions running a million miles a minute.

"Philip, just go," Bri added. "Now," she murmured, "while you still have your face."

His brow bunched again, but he retreated, infuriated as he shoved through the sea of people and disappeared from sight.

Chapter Nine

$\mathcal{R}$aphael turned his eye to Bri, stepping to her and lifting her arm so he could gain a closer look at her wrist.

A harsh expletive flew from his lips. "Are you all right?" His voice brimmed with a dark overtone that rippled throughout her skin.

"Yes." Bri rubbed her wrist. "I'm fine."

He gravitated closer, softly tucking her in an embrace, and looking into her eyes. "I swear to God, I lost you for a second, and—"

"Noo, Raphael, this is my fault—not yours."

Raphael frowned. "*Amour*, don't ever blame yourself for the actions of others." He tucked her chin between his fingers, his gaze boring into hers.

A smile highlighted her face. "I'm not; I just should've reached out to him by now."

"The problem with our society is people assume everything happens on their time, and it doesn't. When you're
ready to have a conversation with him, that's when it will
happen. Trying to force your hand is only going to
force mine."

His threat made her shiver and soaked her panties at the
same time. *Damn.*

"I should get you home."

"No, Raphael, I'm enjoying my time with you here. I
don't want to leave."

Her arms lifted to his neck, wrapping around his shoulders as she made a point to hold him as close as he held her.

"Are you certain?"

Her smile was sweet. "More than ever."

Their heartbeats danced off one another, and in a
smooth sweep, Raphael stepped back into the flow of the
dance, matching the tempo as if it hadn't been disturbed.

"Ladies and gentleman, we are down to the last five
minutes of the night. Hold your loved ones close, and make
sure you have something to toast when the new year
comes in."

Servers streamed through the room, carrying trays of
freshly filled champagne. Still dancing to a groove that only
they could hear, Raphael twirled Bri out, then in again just
as a server paused beside them.

"Champagne, mister, missus," the server said, glancing
between them.

Referencing her as Raphael's missus darkened Bri's
cheeks as heat filled them. She glanced at him, and Raphael
didn't seem to be bothered by it.

"Thank you." Raphael removed two flutes from the tray, handing one over to Bri.

"*Merci,*" she said.

His gaze sparkled as his brow lifted. "*Mon plaisir.*"

My pleasure.

"Two minutes!" Mayor Steele announced over the microphone.

Bri took a sip of her champagne, and Raphael slipped an arm around her, sealing them side by side. She smiled up at him, and he winked down at her and all others in the room braced for the official countdown.

Why Bri's nerves were on edge, she wasn't sure. Maybe because this was the first time she would bring in the new year with someone who made her heart melt. Perhaps it was because it felt right to be in Raphael's arms. Or maybe it was because she didn't want the night to end, and how would he respond if she told him so.

"Thirty seconds!"

Her heart clapped, and slowly she turned in Raphael's arms to face him. Lifting her chin, the dreamy glow in Bri's eyes rocked Raphael's soul.

"Ten, nine, eight, seven!"

The crowd chanted down, and when everyone around them screamed *one,* cheers of "Happy New Year" rang out all over the building. Raphael's warm, firm mouth caressed her forehead in a heated kiss, down the bridge of her nose, to the plush softness of her lips. His mouth melted into hers and stole her gasp of air as the royal blue and black balloons fell from the net they were restrained in across the ceiling. Their arms were tangled in the closest embrace, their bodies, tingling with explicit zest. Heat combed over their face and spread like a display of fireworks.

"Happy New Year, *amour*," he spoke into her mouth.

"Happy New Year," she purred. "You know, if you would like company tonight, I'd love to stay around and maybe…" her words were shy, but she pushed forward, "… hang out for a while." They were enclosed in a furnace of fire, breaths mingling, and pulses invigorated.

Raphael closed his eyes and exhaled, again into her lips. The peppermint on his tongue settled around her mouth, making Bri lick her lips, then his. The erotic flip of her tongue sent heat shooting to his dick, and as if to respond, Raphael's masculinity kicked back against the lower half of her belly.

"When We" by Tank filled the speakers in the room, and as if breaking his resolve, Raphael's mouth covered her lips, his tongue tasting the champagne that rested against her palate. His nostrils flared as he sucked her in so fiercely he almost lost control. His hands gripped her hips, and he pulled her apex against the ridge of his erection, making a sexy purr escape Bri. She wanted it, and Raphael was seconds away from taking her.

"Raphael," she mumbled against his lips. "Let's go upstairs…now."

With uneven breaths, Raphael pulled slowly away to gaze down at her face. His mind whirled, but before he could talk himself out of it, he recaptured her lips, then dropped them, and suddenly, he was walking with Bri's hand in his, leading her through the packed room to the elevators on the other side of the building.

It only took a second for the doors to part and party-goers to mill out as Raphael and Bri moved in. The doors closed, and they jumped each other, Raphael lifting Bri by her ass, her dress easing up generous thighs to bunch around her waist. In his arms, Bri's legs coiled around his abdomen. Their mouths slammed together, hands exploring faces, as they pushed and pulled, sucked and bit, slamming into the wall where Bri was pinned.

Their lips smacked as they kissed, then Raphael dipped his head and sank his tongue into the base of her neck. She hissed as he pulled with a hot suction that made her toes curl and her body vibrate. With his teeth, Raphael pricked her skin, and a growl rumbled from the inner depth of his throat. His hips rotated on a burst of charged chemistry, and his hands dipped down her thighs, coaxing a thread of fire with his incendiary touch. Fingers drove between her thighs, where he caressed her clitoris, instantly recognizing the warmth of silky wet flesh.

He pulled from her neck, his eyes glowing with desire.

"You're not wearing any panties," he said.

Bri's breasts rose and fell as she worked to calm her bated breaths. Her eyes fluttered. "They weren't right for the dress," she whispered, half-shaken and excited, held captive by his predatorial gaze.

Raphael rubbed his fingers together. "You're soaking wet."

"You...you made me this way."

His jaw locked as his orbs circled the breach of her face. Taking the keycard from his inside pocket, Raphael inserted it in the elevators keypad and hit the button for the top floor while keeping his eyes on Bri.

She shivered as he worked while keeping her contact. The elevator began to ascend. "Seven, four, two, three, eight," his thick voice was a deep mutter.

Raphael dipped down to a crouch, and Bri's eyes followed him as his knees sank to the floor. Hot palms patted against the back of her thighs, lifting her with strong fingers that sank into her flesh. Raphael tossed her legs on top of his shoulders and took her labia in his mouth, causing a zing of scorching tingles to flood her body. Writhing, Bri's body bowed like an arrow, her hips thrusting forward, and her head falling back as her body was ambushed with pleasure.

Her mouth opened, eyes wide, while Raphael's hot tongue took hold of her flesh, slurping, licking, and pulling at her sensitized folds.

"Oooh...my God..." Her eyelids fell to half-mast but were stuck on the floor numbers as they lit up on the wall of the elevator cab. With each level they passed, Raphael's consumption drove deeper, exercising a hum like a worshipping chant. Her thighs quaked against his ears, and her hands clutched his head as racing shards of splintering desire ran through every inch of her in circles.

"Oh my God...Raphael..." she whined.

He slurped and massaged her pussy with his tongue nonstop, on a mission to taste the whole of her. She squealed and shut her eyes tight, her teeth gritting as she felt a burst of energy moving through her. The elevator stopped, but they weren't on her floor.

"Oh my Gooood," she moaned, her hips rotating in pleasurable agony, wanting to get away but wanting to be defiled.

"Raphael," she panted.

He responded in the French tongue, but Bri couldn't make out his translation.

"Aaah…oh my God," she moaned and writhed against his mouth while they were stuck in transition, suspended in a globe of passion. "I think…" she panted. "We're stuck… oooh ssss…baby." Her fingers braced against the waves in his hair as his mouth pushed, tongue swirling, in an exploration of her plum.

She was going to come; what if someone tried to gain access to the elevator? Her mind reeled as her hips rocked, her mouth tight when a memory hit her quick.

You're on the top floor with a code so only you can gain access to the floor.

She gasped as if on revelation then remembered the code.

Seven, four, two, three, eight.

Bri's body vibrated, a threatening orgasm on the brink of release. She turned her eyes to the pad of the elevator and reached for the numbers with shaky fingers that thumbed seven, four, two, three, eight.

The jolt in the elevator rising to the top floor shook Bri further, and her head fell back, a moaning shriek tearing from her as crème spilled from her vagina.

Her body twitched as she cried out, rattled like never before.

"Raphael!"

He slurped from her vagina, and her pearl stuck out, pink, taut, and thoroughly aching.

The bell dinged, and Raphael stood, lifting Bri and sweeping her into his arms with an elongated stroll out of the elevator cab.

Down the quiet corridor, he carried her while Bri planted kisses against his neck, jaw, then to his lips. There was no fumble with the key; Raphael entered the suite, and it illuminated upon their entry.

He paused in the doorway and got his first real look at her since her orgasm. Bri's eyes held a heated-desire that mirrored the smolder in Raphael's.

Her hands slipped from his neck and scurried to his belt, unclasping his pants, followed by his zipper. He recaptured her lips, and they fell together in a passionate battle of vivacious vigor.

Swiftly, Raphael pulled away, sucking her lips as he took in a breath. "Shit."

"What's wrong?" Her throaty voice inquired. "Wait, don't answer that."

A heavy breath sailed from his lips. "I don't have a condom." He eyed her with the same intense dark magnitude that rummaged inside him.

"I do," she purred, biting down on his bottom lip. She searched for the cliff of his dick, finding it bent in a hard curve down his leg.

Oh my God.

Her pussy thumped with excited anticipation. Leaning

into him, Bri kissed his lips, enjoying the sweet taste of her canal rich on his mouth. Her hand exercised his shaft that extended up the reach of her arm like an actual third leg.

"*Amour...*" Her lips continued to kiss his face, and neck, then she sucked his ear, conjuring a vibration that rocked through his body.

"Yeah..." she purred, the heat from her mouth coiling around his lobe.

"You should know, I've been celibate for four years." Their gazes locked. "I need you to slow down. I don't want to hurt you."

Their labored breaths moved between their mouths as they stared into the depths of one another's souls.

"Please..." she spoke into his lips. "Hurt me..."

His nocturnal gaze seared her with its poignant stare, and he covered her mouth again just as the pants around his waist hit the floor, lying in a pool around his ankles. Bri yanked the shirt she'd unbuttoned over alpine shoulders and rock-hard arms.

Needing to be inside of her, Raphael took over, discarding his garments then standing Bri on her feet.

"Turn around."

She obeyed, and his fingers unzipped her gown and peeled it from her body. Standing over her, his gaze ate up her brown skin, smooth to the touch and aching with desire.

He kissed her shoulder, a sizzling smooch that ransacked her nerves and made her shiver.

"Are you sure about this?" he asked.

Bri turned around to face him, giving Raphael the first

full look at her rich chocolate skin, hefty breasts, and perky areolas. His dick shot forward, bouncing off her belly in a thumping strike that nearly wounded her stomach. Her pussy clenched as a marching band of nerves joined to meet at her center; pulsating recklessly as her hand reached down to grab his length.

He was fully erect, and Bri had never seen a dick that could do damage until now. She swallowed nervously but still held on to the bravado inside her. Staring at his elongated creation, Bri's mouth watered, and she didn't have to bend far for her lips to meet the head of his dick. Her mouth parted as she eased his cock onto her tongue, sliding her warm lips around his shaft, into the cover of her mouth.

Raphael sucked in a desperate breath, followed by an animalistic sound that created a population of chills down Bri's spine. She sucked hard, then bobbed and weaved, moaning and exuberantly turned on by the erotic entanglement of his shaft. It tasted like a swirl of mint chocolate, coating her tongue and massaging the inner wall of her throat.

"Mmmm," Bri moaned, dropping to her knees. She was under a spell, dripping saliva from the corners of her lips down his erection to the base of his dick. She nodded and sucked, taking his balls in her hand and meeting her fist in a conjoined effort to fill him with pleasure from every angle.

"*Amour...*" He gazed down at her eyes, smoldering and ready to devour her at any second.

"Hmmm? Mmmm..." she asked and moaned simultaneously, sucking, slurping, pulling at his heated dick.

"baise moi..." *fuuuu-ck me...* his dark voice crooned.

Her body tingled, a pack of radiant chills smacked her all at once. She didn't pull away from his dick until he reached down and lifted her from the floor, effortlessly carrying her to the king-size bed in the middle of the suite.

Bri wouldn't admit it, but she was silently shaken. If she were honest with herself, Raphael could murder her tonight in the most blissful death ever.

He laid Bri on her back, and she opened her legs, giving him an eyeful of her fruit. Bri's clitoris was like a protruding thumb, plump and still erect from his suckling mouth. He bent to crawl between her legs, his hands sinking into the mattress, emphasizing the veins that ripped through his muscular arms. His mouth moved to her knees, where he kissed down her thighs, soft and slow. He crossed her apex to kiss above her belly button, rising to wrap his hot mouth over the whole of her breast.

Bri sucked in a breath, her body arching slightly and her head dipping back into the mattress. She didn't see him when Raphael slipped on the condom, but as his tongue danced in a swirl around her nipples, his fingers were expertly covering his shaft.

It was when the head of his dick penetrated her plum did her mouth and eyes widen on a consumption of choked inhalation. His lips moved to her ear as he rose above her while sinking within her canal below. A scattered shower of chills raced over her flesh, and her toes curled as her thighs fell against her stomach, her knees touching her shoulders. He spread her wide, filling her body with the rigid hardness of his cock.

Raphael's eyes dropped then closed, as he took in a lungful of air and steadied his heartbeat.

"You're so hot," he murmured, "so wet... tellement putain humide." *So fucking wet.* He pulled from her ear, his gaze trailing over her mouth up to her eyes.

His first stroke was titanic, pulling out and then plunging in a hot dragging thrust that speared the headboard into the wall and snatched the air from her lungs.

"Aaaah!" Bri's eyes widened.

Raphael paused. "Does it hurt?" he asked.

Bri shook her head but couldn't find her voice, her legs already quaking as her body rejoiced at the rhythmic intensity of his strokes.

"You would tell me if it did, right?"

His hips moved in a grinding tempo, digging into her core where he battered her pussy, thrust for thrust, pound for pound.

Bri bit down on her teeth and nodded.

"Promise me..." He rocked into her harder and slaps between their flesh burned when their skin met.

"Ssss...aaah...yes, Raphael, don't stop, please."

He held her shoulders and lifted into her canal, kissing alongside her face down to her ear. "Promise me," he whispered, slamming into her again.

"I promise!"

She drowned in a pool of heated chills as Raphael rocked the boat, his long strokes discombobulating her on a stimulation of assaulting fervor. Moving from her ear, he captured her mouth, diving his tongue inside as his dick drove between her thighs.

"Mmmm!" She moaned against his tongue, and the room was consumed in reverberating slaps, shouts, and bangs as the headboard continued to slam against the wall.

Bri's body shook, and every time she took a breath, she pulled from his lungs then gave it back as they remained joined on every end.

Seconds ticked into minutes, then Raphael withdrew from her mouth and her pussy simultaneously. His sudden retreat confused her, leaving Bri thirsting for his touch. He flipped her over with one robust turn of his hands, onto her knees, and before Bri could comprehend a response, Raphael's lips were between her ass, stretching his tongue over the mound of her vagina.

"Oooooh!" Bri squealed as his wet muscle flicked against her pointed clitoris. Then with a slurp, he consumed her entire pussy; sucking her folds and satisfying his hunger. "Ooooh my God, baby, baby, bae…"

Her senses were shaken, and her body was combed in sweltering heat.

All at once, Raphael's lips trailed up the hill of her ass, where he sank his mouth into her boasting derriere. He took a bite of her bottom, a growl in his throat as his body vibrated with need.

"Ssss…ooooh…bae…" Bri moaned, taking off in a sprint up the sheets. She tried to get away from him just long enough to regain the control she'd relinquished to his will.

Unfortunately for her, Raphael was one step ahead, and his arm locked her thighs as they coiled around and held her down. Bri continued to squeal as Raphael dipped to her center and took another mouthful of her pussy from the back.

"Oh, my fuckin—"

Her shout was cut when his tongue entered her plum, sweeping with spoonful scoops that added sweet nectar to his palate.

"Oooh my God!"

Her legs vibrated, and her ass clapped as Raphael's tongue traced her pussy to fiddle with the erect nub of her clitoris.

The sensitivity from his hot mouth broke her damn, and Bri screeched as a stream turned into a river within her.

"I'm coming!"

Raphael rose to his knees, entering her sweet heat from behind as his tongue traced up her spine.

"Oooooh!"

Her back arched, and her ass lifted while Raphael's arm circled her waist to keep her in place. His other hand drove up her side over to her breasts where he thumbed her nipple. Her body exploded in an ignition of sparks, and his mouth latched on to the extended arc in her neck.

"Aaah my God, oh my God, Raphael!"

He fucked Bri hard, pounding her pussy so fiercely the headboard beat as if it was bucking to the force of a battering ram.

Her thighs stung as his front connected to her back, igniting more sounds of fierce slaps churning against wet crème. She was losing her mind, her eyes rolling as she braced for each thrust in her womb.

"Oh my God, I'm going to come again!" she shouted.

Raphael tightened his grip, his hips rocking in and out with long catastrophic strokes that threatened to demolish her.

The headboard ricocheted with a fierce whack, drawing a loud pop that caused the wooden plank to splinter as it cracked. The top half fell forward, and with a powerful arm, Raphael caught it before it landed on top of them.

"Oh my God!"

He cuddled Bri in an embrace as he wrestled the remaining pieces apart and tossed the thick wood to the floor.

Their breaths were labored and hearts pounding. Raphael lifted to remove himself from her. "No…" she whispered. "Keep going."

He eyed her from the side, and she nodded, awestruck at his durability.

"Are you sure?" his deep voice drummed, even as he submerged back inside her.

"Yes," she purred. "I want to come again."

Her body vibrated. Crème covered his shaft and slipped down her thighs.

Raphael pummeled to the barricade of her wall, kissing her shoulders down to her neck as he coaxed her mouth to his with the turn of her head. He dug in a milling stroke, whining his hips and burying his dick in an exhibition to pull another orgasm from her. He tweaked her nipples back and forth with one hand while eating her mouth and feeding her pussy with his raging cock. Her body quaked again.

"Oh, God…"

Raphael's lips dropped to her chin, and his hips rocked,

picking up momentum as he lifted one leg, dipping and digging, grinding and milling, pounding and popping.

"*Tu es tellement incroyable… tellement putain incroyable.*" *You're so amazing… so fuckin amazing,* his gruff voice murmured. His hips were in an upsurge, and his orgasm on edge.

"Aah, yes, yes, yes! I'm coming again. My God, my God in heaven, my God!" she screamed.

His drive excelled to supersonic levels, and their skin burned from the fever of their conjoining spirited brushes.

"*Viens avec moi…*" he murmured.

Come with me.

Their mouths crashed as their tongues clashed, and together, they rocked into an orgasm that sent them spinning and moaning, clamped down in a tightly fierce hold.

Bri's ears popped, and her entire body quaked as her eyes rolled.

Hot tingles ran through them both, and as if Bri was falling off a cliff, the rigidness in her limbs unlocked, causing her lips to slip away from his. Her head dropped to the bed, and her pussy thumped recklessly as crème continued to drown his dick.

"Oh my God, oh my God, oh my God," she murmured. Hot kisses—velvety, firm, and moist—pressed against the center of her back, pouncing in a crawl up her spine. Her body continued to quake, and when Raphael exited her canal, a whimper fell from Bri's lips.

He cuddled her in his arms, turning her to face him where she snuggled in the nook of his neck.

"You are so very amazing, *amour….*"

He kissed her forehead and spread those caresses to her

temples; one side then the other. Down the bridge of her nose, his mouth brushed her, and when he made it to her lips, the flow of her soft breathing made him cock his head and eye her. A subtle smile trekked across his lips.

Bri was fast asleep.

Chapter Ten

She could've slept all day, but something in her spirit stirred Bri awake, and as her eyes fluttered open, they were met with a dark bluish gaze.

"Good morning."

The strum of his vocals rippled through her, making a squirm inevitable. A smile eased across her lips.

"Good morning," she responded. She stretched, arms over her head, as she untangled her limbs from his and extended her legs. "Was I snoring?"

Raphael chuckled. "Soft snores. Easy, like a resting baby."

Her smile lifted into her eyes just as Bri realized she probably had morning breath.

"Oh God," she said, turning her back to him and sliding across the bed, taking the thick sheets with her.

"What's wrong?" he asked, alarmed.

"Oh, um, I probably should freshen up before I get back in your face." It was then that she eyed him. "Speaking of freshening up, why does your breath smell like Colgate?"

Raphael laughed. "I've been up for a while."

She turned to him fully, staying perched on the other side of the bed with the sheets lifted to cover her body as if he hadn't done ungodly things to her last night. It was then that she noticed he was dressed. The black tailored jacket was tossed on a desk chair in the corner of the room. But he was wearing his shirt. It was opened at the collar, showing the masculine frame of his neck, but it wasn't tucked in, instead, it stretched over his pants and ruffled at the edges.

"Do you need to leave?"

"No. I couldn't get back to sleep."

"Tell the truth, I was snoring, wasn't I? That's why you couldn't go back to sleep."

Raphael laughed. "No, silly girl. I awakened to use the bathroom, and I've been up ever since." He paused. "Watching you."

A blush fell over Bri.

She loved hearing the soft trace of desire in his voice; it made her wonder if things between them could go farther. Raphael reached over to her, wrapping his arms around Bri's waist and pulling her in a slide back across the bed. The masculinity of him blanketed her in thick waves of heat, coating a population of chills to the soles of her feet.

"*Amour...*" His gaze draped over her, and he reached out to grasp her hand. "Last night was...beautiful." He pulled her closer. "You're beautiful." His hands lifted to her neck, then slipped up to cup her face. "If you don't mind, will you have breakfast with me?"

Bri was elated. "Of course. You didn't think I was gonna hit it and quit it, did you?"

Raphael's mouth spread, and his eyes sparkled on a roaring wave of laughter.

Her heart fluttered as her body continued to melt under the intense warmth of his ambiance.

He stood and held out his hand.

"Come."

Her hand slipped into his brawny palm, and Raphael helped her off of the bed.

"One stop in the bathroom, and I'll be ready in thirty minutes."

"Does that mean an hour?" he asked.

Bri smiled and sank her hand against her hips, steadying herself for a snarky retort. Instead, she grinned. "Maybe."

Shrugging, she then turned and left with Raphael's laughter lingering behind her.

"MMMM," BRI LIFTED HER NOSE TO THE AIR. "IT SMELLS like homemade pancakes and freshly brewed coffee in here."

Raphael's mouth eased into a handsome grin. "It does."

They were seated inside Cozy Corner Restaurant, a pancake house located in Chicago's Edgewater district. When they arrived, the couple was seated quickly, and within two minutes, a waitress had taken their order and left to retrieve their cup of brew.

"I didn't get a chance to express before we left how amazing last night was," Bri said.

Raphael's gaze turned into one of longing, a flicker of determination in the strength of his eyes.

"I hope I didn't scare you with the headboard incident." He paused. "That's a first."

Bri's giggle was deep in her throat, a hearty beat that made his body tingle.

"It wasn't the only thing you tore up," she murmured under her breath.

"What was that?"

"Huh?"

"What was that last thing you just said."

"Hmm, me? I don't recall."

Raphael's gorgeous mouth lifted, and he bit his lip. "Sure you don't," he teased.

Bri shrugged, a whimsical smirk on her face.

The waitress returned with steaming coffee, and the vapors released a sweet morning aroma into the air.

"I bet this coffee is delicious." Bri blew over the top and inhaled the brew's fresh scent.

"You should hold your tongue before taking a sip," Raphael warned.

"I don't wanna." Her brows wiggled, and that brought a light chuckle from Raphael.

"If you don't, you'll wish you had."

"Okay, you've made your case." Bri pushed away from the cup, sitting back against her seat. She crossed her legs and focused on Raphael's lips, which made her mind fill with every delicious thing he'd accomplished with that mouth. Her naughty thoughts morphed when a memory of Philip demanded her attention. The last thing she would ever want was to see Raphael distressed, or incensed, and last night—Philips antics had done just that.

"What's on your mind?" Raphael asked.

All of Bri's life, she'd been connected to others, feeling their sadness, their joys, discomforts, and pains. It was just like breathing, and when she was younger, Bri always wondered why that was. Finding out she was an empath didn't give her the shock she thought it would. It was Bri's way of life, so she embraced it as she grew.

Throughout that time, no one had come close to reciprocating her sentiments, but that had changed since meeting Raphael. Her eyes lingered in the window of his gaze as they sat in quiet pause.

"I've got to decide on the direction Building Bridges will go."

He nodded. "What are you thinking?"

Bri cleared her throat. "First, I need to have a serious conversation with Philip, and depending on how that goes, I'll know how to move forward."

The structure of Raphael's face changed as his jaw tightened, his mind racing over last night's debacle on the dance floor.

"Has he ever put his hands on you before?"

"No." Her brows furrowed. "It was unlike him."

"You should take your company back and disassociate yourself with him. He's trouble."

"I know what it looked like, but it's not like that at all. He's actually a caring guy."

"*Amour...*"

"Okay, so I know how that sounds, but it's not what you think, seriously. Philip was just upset and rightfully so. I'm sure it was just a heat of the moment type of thing. You know sometimes things can happen quick—"

"Please..." Raphael shook his head. "Don't."

Bri closed her lips, her plea seemingly having no effect on the matter.

"I want you to understand something. It is never okay to be assaulted under any circumstances. Period."

"You're overreacting."

"I don't think that I am."

Bri sighed. She didn't want to keep going down this conversational road.

"Let's talk about something else." She lifted her coffee.

"Do you plan to meet with him again?"

Bri huffed. "You make it sound like we're dating."

"Are you?"

"No!" She set her coffee down. "I wouldn't be with you if we were."

Raphael exhaled. "I'm sorry. I was wrong." He paused. "I'm just trying to understand why you're taking up for his actions."

"We work together. We're partners. He's a good guy, most of the time."

Raphael couldn't help but feel that there was something more.

"Is there anything else I should know?"

"Like what?" She crossed her legs, her posture changing in her seat.

Raphael sat back against his chair, eyeing her body language. She was on alert and a little anxious, and as he studied her, Bri folded her arms and gazed out of the window. Her change in disposition gave him pause, and he knew then there was some greater attachment between Bri and Philip.

"I apologize if I upset you." He paused. "It's none of my business."

Bri sighed and turned back to him. "Raphael."

"It's okay," he said, lifting his coffee and taking a much-needed swig. "I'm out of order. You don't owe me any explanation. Please, accept my apology."

Bri shifted in her seat, uncomfortable about the turn of conversation.

"Let's talk about the charity race," Raphael said. "We'll need to practice for the obstacle course. I say we should meet up at least twice before the race. Although we want to win, if we make it to second or third place, the charity will still receive a donation."

He sounded devoid of emotion like they were in a business meeting among colleagues.

The waitress reappeared with their food, and after she was gone, the table remained quiet. "Do you mind if we pray?" Raphael asked.

She shook her head instead of using her voice, and Raphael reached across the table and pulled her hands into his.

He blessed their food while giving praise to God, and Bri silently willed her thoughts to stay focused on his petition and not the warmth of his fingers. When he released her hand, it was only then that she realized it was over.

There were no words between them as they ate, with only the clang of silverware to the dishes making any noise.

Thirty minutes into the meal, Raphael's dish had barely been touched, and Bri was feeling like a fool.

"How's your food?" Raphael asked, checking his watch.

"It's pretty good." She glanced over his then eyed him. "How's yours?"

He smiled, but it wasn't refreshing, simply a polite thing to do with no meaning behind it.

"Same," he said.

"How would you know? You've barely touched it."

"I've had my share."

The table quieted down. "I think I'm done," Bri said.

"Are you sure?"

"Yeah…"

"In that case, I'll get the check." He turned to find the waitress.

"Raphael…" She paused as his gaze drifted back to hers. "I apologize." She sighed. "I don't want us to leave today with anything between us. I recognize that you're just looking out for me, and I appreciate it. I…" She paused again then sighed. "I have my reasons for wanting to work things out with Philip. But I want you to understand I'm not involved with him in any way except through our shared business."

Raphael eyed her a moment longer. "You didn't have to explain that."

"Yes, I did. I enjoy my time with you, and the last thing I

want is for anything to be misinterpreted between us. Will you accept my apology?"

His face warmed. "I do. Can I ask a favor of you?"

"Sure."

"When you meet up with him again, do it in public." Before she could object, he added, "Just to make sure his head is on straight."

A soft smile lingered on Bri's lips. "I can do that."

Raphael folded his hands in prayer. "*Merci.*"

The waitress sidled up to the table. "Are you ready for the check?"

Raphael eyed her. "I believe we are." His gaze shifted to Bri for confirmation.

"We are," Bri said.

"The lady says we are," Raphael added with a grin. He winked over at Bri St. James, and she winked back.

Chapter Eleven

Six days later

"*W*ait! He broke the headboard?"

Allison's eyes bugged as she tried to keep up with Bri's pace.

Bri nodded. "I was terrified and turned on at the same damn time."

Allison laughed as the wind around them slapped her face while they ran. "Ooooh, sheeeet!" Allison cursed. "That man must have been buried in frustration." She shook her head. "Are your insides still intact because I have a great gynecologist who may be able to check you out and see."

That tickled Bri to pieces just as Allison ran out of breath and dropped to her knees, huffing, and puffing.

I think my ovaries were getting into place."

Allison peered at Bri. "Say what now?"

Bri nodded. "Girl, everything inside my womb shifted. I think I'm gonna have his babies."

Allison's eyes widen as her mouth drop. "Are you serious!?" Laughter escaped Allison's mouth.

"Allison, you're laughing, but you didn't feel how my organs moved girl." Bri rested her palms against her stomach. "The weirdest part about it is how down I feel about it. Like I'd birth his empire."

Allison's laughter continued to shriek.

"Girl, my body is still buzzing from the experience, and now I yearn for his touch. No one, and I mean no one, has ever made me feel so deliciously sated."

"Wooo chile, I bet, but you're with a Valentine now; get used to it." They laughed, still out of breath. "I thought you preferred to run inside during colder months."

"I do." Bri bent with Allison but rested in a crouch on her feet.

"Then why in the world are we out here in freezing temperatures?"

"Girl, I wouldn't call forty-nine degrees freezing temperatures."

Allison's brows furrowed. "You're kidding, right? Do you feel Jack Frost slipping up the crack of your ass, 'cause I do!"

Bri shook her head. "What's wrong with you acting all out of shape?"

"I'll tell ya. It's cold as all get out, *and* my bones have been relaxed because for the past seven days my husband's worked every muscle that makes up my skeleton."

Bri shouted in laughter, then covered her mouth, tickled to death as the amusement slipped through her.

She spread her fingers. "Okay! That's nice!"

Allison nodded. "It is."

"You're so in love, I think I envy that."

"Let me tell you something, if you knew what I knew, maybe you would." Allison laughed, and Bri shook her head again. "But then again, you've got Splinter over there tearing up your furniture; maybe you shouldn't."

Their cackling continued.

"It wasn't my furniture. It was The Drake Hotel's."

"Don't they have expensive stuff? No way that head-board should've broken."

Bri shrugged. "I don't think it had a choice."

"Sheeet!" Allison cursed again, being silly with her expletive terminology.

They were at Chicago's lakefront trail getting their last run for the week out of the way. In workout gear, head-bands, and timed wristwatches, the two women had taken on a four-mile sprint. However, being that their initial goal was six miles, they still had two remaining.

"Wooo, girl, I don't know if I can go another two miles," Allison complained.

"Come on, I need you to finish this with me."

"Why, Jesus?" Allison asked, clutching her imaginary pearls.

"Because this charity race is a three-mile obstacle course."

From the moment they'd linked up, Allison and Bri had been discussing the last two weeks, and Bri revealed everything except for the awkwardness between her and Raphael at breakfast the day after their amazing sex. Over the past few days, Bri's conversation with Raphael was there one day, gone the next. On the days she didn't hear from him, she worried unnecessarily, but it was a part of her character to be concerned about his state of mind.

Allison held up her hands and counted her fingers, her eyes crossing as she came to a conclusion. "That's three miles less than your goal today, what am I missing?"

"All we're doing is running. So I figured if I have enough stamina to run six miles, I can survive a three-mile obstacle course."

"And so you decided to kill me along with yourself." Allison snapped her fingers. "Got it."

"Don't be like that."

"No, don't *you* be like that."

"It's like you said, you need the workout anyway since you've been on your ass the past week. Literally." Bri laughed.

Allison snorted. "I never said nothing of the sort."

"So you didn't say you've been getting waxed all week?"

"I wasn't talking about that part. I was talking about the need-to-work-out-because-of-it part."

Bri laughed and shook her head.

"If you needed to practice so bad, why didn't you drag Raphael out here with you? He's the one that needs to be here."

When Bri didn't respond, Allison eyed her closely.

"Ahem," she said. "Did you hear what I just said?"

"*Yeah,* I heard you." Bri fumbled with her bottom lip,

flipping the plump flesh in and out of her mouth. "The thing is, I think he may be upset with me."

Allison frowned and stood from the ground. "Why would he be upset?"

Bri fumbled with her lip some more and then told Allison about the change in tone in their conversation at breakfast after Raphael suggested that Philip was trouble.

"Let me guess, you folded yo' lil arms and legs, then puckered your lips, and tuned him out, correct?"

Allison was bewildered. The only person Bri was known to ignore a person over completely was Philip, and that was because Philip, reminded Bri of her brother Dean St. James. However, whenever Allison would bring up this unsettling issue, Bri would do to Allison what she'd done to Raphael, fold her arms, and pout; then completely ignore Allison and the subject at hand.

"I didn't mean to. You know how I am about Dean."

"Except this isn't Dean we're talking about here, Bri, this is Philip."

Bri sighed. "I meant Philip." She tossed her hands in the air. "This is why I skipped this particular part of the conversation this morning."

"So I wouldn't put you in check because you know that I will?"

"Whatever."

"No, seriously. If you want me to run these two miles with you, we're having a come-to-Jesus moment right now."

Bri pursed her lips and folded her arms. "I already know what you're going to say."

Allison just stared at her friend for a long minute. "Then why do you keep doing this to yourself?"

Bri opened her mouth.

"You know what, scratch that. Stop doing this to yourself."

Bri didn't respond; instead, she walked to a park bench and sat down. The tree hovering overhead waved as the wind ruffled its leaves, and Allison folded her arms and rubbed her shoulders.

"Bri…" Allison approached her and sat down next to her friend. "What do I need to do to help you?"

"I don't need help."

"Okay, for just two minutes, listen to what I have to say and tell me how it sounds. You have a friend whom you consider a sister and care about the best interests of her heart. You met her in junior high school and found out she had a sexy brother, too."

"My brother is so not sexy," Bri responded with an eyebrow arch.

"Shush, I'm telling a story. This isn't about you. It's about *your friend*, remember?"

Bri tightened the fold of her arms and listened.

"You and your friend and her brother basically grew up together, caught the school bus, argued and fought like normal friends and siblings, but your friend's brother always takes up for her. If anyone has anything to say or wants to try and harm her in any way, your friend's brother is there to protect her."

Allison shifted her butt on the bench and crossed her legs.

"You witness their relationship and how close they are and wish you yourself had a brother that acted the same way. Then when her brother turns twenty-six, he enrolls in the United States Army. He does it without mentioning it to anyone but his father because he's trying to impress dear ol' dad." Allison saw the expression on Bri's face plummet with melancholy.

"When he's accepted, the news spreads throughout the community before he can get a chance to tell his friends, family, or his girlfriend. It hits the local newspapers first, and everyone is affected in different ways.

"Your friend's father is excited, proud, and congratulatory when he finds out. Her mother is also proud but shocked and worried all at the same time. His girlfriend's heart is broken, and she feels betrayed and now also worried. But the person that's most affected is your friend. She doesn't tell you, but you see the change in her immediately."

This time it was Bri that shifted, the words spoken by Allison uncomfortable as they settled in her spirit.

"You catch her crying at times when she thinks no one's around. Your hangout sessions are cut to a minimum. She makes the decision to transfer from the local college to attend a university outside of the state when the plans were always for you to graduate from the same university together.

"Then when she comes back, not only is she all grown-up, but she's found another friend. Someone who resembles her brother. He even has the same haircut and minimal facial hair. They're the same height, build, complexion. The guy could probably play him in a movie if the need ever arose.

"All of a sudden, your friend gives him a part of her business, she allows him to handle the finances, and trusts him as if she's known him all her life. She really thinks it's just a harmless friendship, but you aren't blind. The guy's in love with her and does whatever she wants to prove it, but she still can't see it because she only sees what she has wanted to see. Her brother." Allison's direct tone softened as she sympathized with Bri.

"At first, you thought it was cute, but then you start to worry because your friend is now allowing him to run her over, and you know she's blinded by the love for her brother.

"When your friend's brother suddenly stops calling for years on end, your friend's anxiety shoots through the roof because now she's afraid that something gruesome has happened to him.

"You're worried about her brother, too, but you want to show your friend how dangerous the situation is that she's in.

"What do you do, Bri?"

Bri's eyes watered, but she held the tears in check.

"Please tell me, how do you help your friend?"

Bri wiped her eyes and sniffed. Her jaw locked then released as she took in a haggard breath. "I miss him so much, Allison." The waterworks started almost immediately, and Allison threw her arms around Bri as Bri turned her head and wept on Allison's shoulder.

"I know you do. More than anything, but you've got to understand, baby, Philip is not Dean. He never will be, and I know you hate to hear this, but he is using you. You gotta let him go."

"I don't know how to do that." Bri lifted her head and wiped her eyes. "Where is he, Allison? Why hasn't Dean called or reached out to us? I can't help but think—"

"I know, and I also know when a member of the military dies, their family receives a notice. You all haven't gotten anything like that, have you?"

"No, but it makes no sense. Why wouldn't he contact us?"

"I don't know, baby. I wish I did. But listen to me, whatever the reason, it has to be a good one. I will help you reach out to somebody, anybody in the military who can let us know that he's okay. Even if it takes years, I'm going to do that for you because I love you, and I love Dean."

Bri eyed her. "Seriously?"

"Yes, girl. If I'd have known you wanted to do this, we would've done it already, but you were so good with acting as if everything was fine and looking to take care of others."

"I'm an empath—"

"Yeah, yeah, I know, but even empaths need someone."

Bri sighed. "Thank you."

"Don't thank me yet."

Bri groaned.

"Yeah, it's coming." Allison pursed her lips then sighed. "You've got to get rid of Philip." She felt Bri stiffen. "At first, I thought he was good for you, but Bri, the guy loves you, and you see him through a completely different lens."

"Do you really think he's—"

"Yes, honey, Stevie Wonder can see it. You're the only one who can't."

Bri let out an exasperated breath. "What am I supposed to say, get out of my life? That's rude."

Allison shook her head. "There you go again, worried about everyone else. Look, you're going to put your business hat on and tell him why you two can no longer work together. He stole from your company, he assaulted you on the dance floor—"

"It wasn't…"

Bri closed her lips at the peer of Allison's steady stare.

"Bri."

"You're right." Bri dropped her head in her hands. "I'll do it."

"When?"

"I don't know, in a couple of days."

"No, Bri."

"What?"

"That'll only give you time to talk yourself out of it."

Bri sighed. "I'll do it tomorrow."

"Promise me."

"What are we, children?"

"Promise me and stop beating around the bush."

Bri sighed again. "Fine, I promise." Bri took in a heavy breath. "What about Raphael?"

"If you want him—and I don't mean as a friend, either—you'll tell him why you reacted the way you did."

They sat in silence, watching as other runners jogged the trail. Bri slipped a loose strand of hair that was swaying across her eyes back behind her ear.

"It is a little nippy out here," Bri said.

Allison scoffed. "You still want to run those two miles?"

"I guess I can give you a break. Besides, I'm meeting up with Raphael tomorrow for our first practice session."

"Perfect timing."

Bri peered at Allison. "You think I should bring it up then?"

"Why wouldn't you?"

Bri held back her response as she thought about it. She shrugged. "I just assumed that wouldn't be the time for it."

"Girl, please, when is the time?"

"I don't know, dinner, maybe?"

"Are you going to ask him out on a date?"

"I could."

"Tell him before you begin your session. That way it's all out in the open, and you guys can really focus on what you're doing."

Bri nodded.

"Now, let's get something warm to drink. I think a cup of cappuccino would do." Allison pulled her phone from the strapped band around her waist.

"Who are you calling?"

Allison glanced to Bri as her finger continued to work the screen. "A Lyft."

"For what?"

Allison's head swayed side to side. "So we can get back to our cars four miles down the road."

Bri's mouth dropped. "You're calling a ride-sharing service when we can walk or run for that matter?"

"It's four miles!" Allison shrugged. "This is your lane, not mine; so don't judge me."

Bri just stared at her friend. She loved her death, but the girl was something else.

The next day

BRI RUSHED THROUGH THE SWINGING DOOR IN A HURRY TO escape the frigid winds. Her plight carried her to a desk where a tall Caucasian male in a tank top and headband stood behind a station. He looked the part of a skilled instructor, wearing the workout gear with arms packed with muscles sprouting from his torso.

When he glanced up at Bri, a smile surfaced across his face, and Bri could tell even with his strong physique that he was in his early fifties by the maturity behind his gaze.

"Good morning, how can I help you, young lady?"

"I'm here for a session with Raphael Valentine."

"Bri St. James?" the man asked.

"Yes." Her eyes lit up. "Am I late or something? I wrote down the time."

"No, you're fine. Mr. Valentine is waiting for you in the storm room downstairs." The man came from behind the counter with a hand held out.

"I'm Barry, it's nice to meet you. If you'll follow me, I'll take you to him."

"Okay, thanks."

He nodded. "This way."

They strolled down a corridor going in the opposite
direction of the main gym, past a few offices, to an elevator
at the rear of the building.

They entered and rode down to the bottom floor; all the
while, Bri wondered why they were working out in a
storm room.

When the ride ended on the ground floor, the doors
opened to a cemented, brick-built in room that was
rectangular in length and currently set up like a makeshift
obstacle course.

Bri's eyes widened as they walked off the elevator into
the area, moving past three sets of monkey bars hanging
high over a safety net that Raphael was currently securing.
Her eyes had a mind of their own as they rode over the cut
in his muscular arms, thick biceps, and the solid pillar of his
throat. From his side profile, Raphael's groomed beard was
always perfectly aligned down his strong jaw, teasing the
underline of his lips. She remembered the way those lips felt
on her skin. So hot, firm, moist—spellbinding.

A shudder ran through Bri as her eyes continued down
the strength of his design and the tautness of his ass. A
black tank top covered the expanse of his back and spandex
shorts crept from underneath a pair of close-fitting basket-
ball shorts. She noticed the fingerless gloves fitted on his
hands and made a mental note to buy some herself.

"Knock, knock," Barry said.

Raphael glanced over, his fingers still gripping the straps
to check their resilience.

A lazy grin covered his mouth as his gaze rested on Bri,
and in return, she also smiled.

"You have a visitor," Barry announced.

Raphael took a hard tug on the net, then released it and turned to Barry with a hand held out.

"Thank you for showing Ms. St. James down," Raphael said.

"Not a problem. If you need me, just holler."

"Will do."

Barry left the room, exiting the same way he came. Raphael dropped his hands to his waist, his gaze trailing over Bri from head to toe. She was dressed also in tight-fitting spandex, but Raphael couldn't get a good look at the garment due to the oversized cotton shirt that covered her torso down to the curve in her hips.

"Good morning," Raphael's greeted.

"Good morning."

"It looks like you came almost prepared."

Bri glanced over herself. "Uh oh, what did I do wrong?"

Raphael's easy smile melted her bones.

"I wouldn't say it's wrong, just a small adjustment will get you together." He stepped into her space, so close she could smell the aftershave on his skin. "Do you mind?" he asked, his hands moving to the hem of her shirt.

"Um, no, not at all."

"This is a bodysuit underneath your top, correct?"

He was leaned into her face in a semi-crouch, which was needed to bring himself to her height and lift the garment. Bri's heart knocked, and damn it if her nipples didn't harden right then.

"Yes." She swallowed. "It is."

He nodded, and removed her shirt, with Bri holding her

arms up and taking in a breath as a tingling vibration arrested her. The move sent sexually charged tension racing between them. They acknowledged the chemistry as they both paused, him staring into her brown irises and biting his bottom lip as she stared back, transfixed on his mouth.

"There," he said. "Cotton is your worst enemy in a sport like this. It'll only weigh you down if it gets wet."

Bri's heart fumbled like an old-time rickety alarm clock, her mind stuck on his last word: *wet*.

"Wet?"

"Yeah." He pulled back to his six feet three inches, a tiny smile cornering his lip. "Some courses have surprises, and while I have the basic map of what we'll meet when the race begins, the organizers have decided to keep the couples race a secret. So, who knows what we'll be getting into once we're faced with it? Let me show you what we are looking to come up against, and then we can begin."

Bri nodded and stepped in line with his stride.

"When the diagram of the race was released, I took the liberty to set up this one here. It matches as close to the obstacles you'll face for the women's run."

"The women's run?"

"Yes." Raphael stopped at the wall in the back of the room. "The race is made up of three courses. "The men's, the women's, then the final course, which is the couple's course."

"Interesting. How does it work?"

"The race will start with the women's race."

"Of course," she teased.

Raphael smiled. "I'm confident that you will do well."

"Thanks, but how do you know?"

His dark voice scurried across her skin when he spoke. "You're in shape, and your flexibilities are endless."

Heat scorched Bri's cheeks, stinging her face, and without thinking about her next words, she blurted, "I have upper body strength, too."

Raphael's gaze pierced her, so intense she could've melted into the wall behind her. His voice was gruff when he spoke.

"I don't doubt it." He cleared his throat and forced himself to focus. "That's why I know you will be fine." He reached out to her and pinched her chin.

"It starts with a one-mile run—" Raphael walked as he talked, "—that will turn into these challenges you see before you." In front of them, ten large black tires outlined their pathway. Bri nodded as her mind conjured a program she'd seen on TV, with soldiers dashing through the tires on a drill. The thought instantly made her think of Dean, and suddenly, a wave of sadness covered her.

"It will also end in a one mile sprint to the finish line. The course is small, but the obstacles will take this upper body strength you say you have." He turned to her with a smile, but it fell as he sensed her grief.

He paused his stride. "Is there anything wrong?"

Doing her best to hide her gloom, Bri lifted her shoulders and held her chin up, her eyes meeting his.

"I'm fine." She cleared her throat and got back on topic. "It's the monkey bars that will test me, right?" She smirked, but Raphael could see behind her phony smile.

He eyed her with a gaze that caressed her soul and made

Bri want to spill her silent thoughts. "I can't help but notice that you're quick to offer an aiding hand when you feel someone is distressed while just as quick to keep your frustrations buried. Talk to me."

Bri sighed. She wasn't used to being transparent to another person, and her jaw locked at the thought of her brother's absence being something she would have to live with for the rest of her life.

"I actually do want to speak with you about last week."

As they stood side by side, Raphael turned to face her.

"I want to apologize for the way I acted over breakfast regarding Philip. Truth is…" She paused and rubbed her hands together nervously.

His gaze dropped to her fingers then drifted back to her face.

"*Amour…*" His brows dipped. "Take a deep breath for me." His arms lifted and reached to grip her shoulders.

Bri did as he asked, her smile uneasy. "This shouldn't be so difficult for me to express, but in all honesty, I've never faced my own issues." Her eyes dropped to her hands.

"Take your time."

She smiled up at him. "Thanks." She sighed. "Six years ago, my brother Dean enrolled in the United States Army. He was twenty-six and apparently looking to make our father proud. Throughout our youth, we were like most siblings, nitpicking about everything but best friends at the same time." She smiled, but it faded just as fast. "Some would say we were as thick as thieves, and outside of our relationship, we had few friends. Allison was one of mine and his high school sweetheart was one of his.

"When the news broke that he was going to the Army, it blindsided many of us close to him. Me, especially. But instead of facing that truth, I hid it, only allowing it to come out when I would cry at night when no one could hear me."

Raphael's features relaxed as he kept a calm eye resting on Bri, his heart now tap-dancing in his chest.

"I felt like I needed to start fresh, so I dumped my plans to graduate college here in Chicago and enrolled at Clark Atlanta University. Once there, I did feel a sense of renewal, and I embraced campus life full throttle, putting my focus on building my education so I could start my business. Well..." Her hands fidgeted again. "...that's where I met Philip. He and I hit it off pretty quickly and not in the way you think. Our friendship was instant. We were calling each other best friends before the first semester ended." She swallowed.

"For me, life was okay, I'd get calls every blue moon from Dean. Whenever he had the opportunity to reach out to us, he did. That was nice, but it didn't fill the void I had for my little brother." She sighed. "I didn't realize it at the time, but I'd internally substituted Philip for Dean. I first noticed their similarities when we were at a Jay-Z and Beyoncé concert.

"Philip was wearing a Rocawear jersey with his hands held high as he threw up the Roc hand sign. Everything about his persona reminded me of Dean in that instant, and it gave me a moment of pause and obvious surprise because I'd never seen it before then. I immediately became saddened and cried in the middle of the concert." Bri attempted to shake off her despair with a wiggle of her shoulders.

"After about three years, I no longer heard from Dean." Her eyes watered. "I don't know why he stopped reaching out to us. I'd call my mother and ask, but neither she nor my father had received contact. I began to worry, but my parents weren't as concerned. He'll call when he can, they would say."

Bri focused in on Raphael's gaze; it lingered softly without disrupting the masculine edge of his features.

"I drew closer to Philip, but still I could feel the void." She sighed. "When you questioned our relationship status, honestly, it felt nauseating because I could never see him as anything other than a friend. But I do understand now how our situation looks, and I wanted you to know that I'm working on fixing that."

"*Amour*, I meant no harm and sincerely apologize if I offended you. I make no excuses for my query. It wasn't my place to begin with."

"That's just it, Raphael. When you and I were together on New Year's Eve, I felt something more come out of the time we spent with one another. My attraction to you has always been there, but spending that night in your arms connected us on a spiritual level that I can't put into words. At least for me, it did. So yeah, I think you had a right to ask, especially if..." she shrugged, "...if you felt the same way."

Raphael exhaled. "Feel," he corrected. At Bri's bunched brows, he elaborated. "You said felt, past tense. But there's

STEPHANIE NICOLE NORRIS

nothing past about the emotion settling within me because it's happening right now the longer we stand here."

Bri's heart thumped, and her pulse picked up a double dose of speed.

"My apology still stands. If I had given you time, maybe you would've told me about this when you were ready."

"I'm ready now, which is why I'm telling you. It still boggles me that I tried to ignore it for so long. Mainly because I didn't want it to be true."

"I understand, and I'd like to fill some of that void if you allow me to." He reached for her hand and caressed her fingers. "I don't have all the answers, but I'm willing to help you search for Dean, and I'd like us to remain...close if that's all right with you."

Her heart did jumping jacks, and a smile rose into her eyes.

"I'd like that very much."

Raphael bit his bottom lip then pulled her into the width of his torso for a body-hugging torrid embrace. Resting against the column of his throat, Bri sighed, suddenly rejuvenated and ready to embrace the day as her arms held tightly to his cut body.

"Would you like to reschedule today? We can take a walk and talk if you'd prefer?"

"No way." Bri pulled back, lifting her eyes to his. "We've got work to do. The race is next week, and we're going to win this thing."

A gorgeous smile spread across Raphael's face, and he winked. "Yeah, we are." He coached her to his side, and they walked the few feet back to the tires.

"We're going to start here."

"The easiest way to tackle this is to step one foot in, one foot out."

He released her and demonstrated, hopping through the tires like a trained athlete. At the end, he returned the run, sprinting with ease through the rubber loops.

"You ready to give it a go?"

Bri nodded. "You made it look so easy."

"That's because it is."

"I'll be the judge of that when this is over."

Raphael's husky laugh warmed her body as she strolled to stand in front of the tires. His gaze fell to the timer on his wrist. "On three," he said.

Bri planted her feet with a wide semi-bend to her knees.

"Three!"

She took off, jumping through the tires, one after the other. When she made it to the end, Bri spun around and headed back without pause until she'd made it out of the last tire.

"Great job!" he boasted, his hand lifted for a high five.

She beamed, taking in a few quick breaths as their hands slapped midair. "Thank you. I was so nervous."

He pulled her in and tweaked her chin.

"You are going to blow this thing out of the water."

Her grin extended, and suddenly, her confidence was boosted.

"You might be on to something, Raphael."

He winked down at her. "Of course I am."

She smirked.

"Next," he said, "the monkey bars."

Chapter Twelve

When Bri strolled into her studio apartment, it took pure determination to walk to her shower and force herself into the tub. To say she was exhausted was an understatement.

But as the water beat over her shoulders, the only thing she could think about was Raphael. They went through the course again and again, tackling the obstacles that were the most troubling. The monkey bars weren't so bad, but if there were more than six in a row, Bri worried her upper body strength would give out.

That wasn't the half of it. The rope climb also tested her upper body strength, and each time she tried it, Bri plummeted to the safety net.

"That's okay, we'll do it again, and you'll get it," Raphael encouraged.

But really there was no *we* that needed to get it together.

It was just Bri. After watching Raphael take the course head-on with simplistic ease, it only added to the mound of pressure she began to feel. However, Bri was determined to win, and on their next meet up in three days, she would make sure to excel through them all.

Deciding she needed a relaxing bath, Bri added her essential oils and bubbles to the tub and switched off the shower nozzle. Thirty minutes into her warm reservoir, Bri was nodding off to sleep, but her phone rang, pulling her from the haze of a dream that was destined to pull her under.

Bri's eyes shifted to the sink, where her discarded iPhone rested at the edge. She leaned for it, arms outstretched and fingers bicycling for a sturdy grip.

Getting it within her grasp, Bri glanced at the screen then answered on the second ring.

"Hey, girl," she said into the line.

"Hey, I didn't catch you at a bad time, did I?" Allison asked.

"I'm in a bubble bath if you call that a bad time."

"Nah," Allison said, "unless Raphael is in there with you."

Bri laughed. "How I wish. I've dreamed of us in this exact position, with me in front of him getting a shoulder massage. I could use that right now, too."

"Damn, now I want one."

They laughed with low sultry giggles.

"I didn't call to hold you. I just wanted to make sure you were okay after your conversation with Philip. You didn't call, but I didn't want to interrupt."

Bri fell suddenly quiet, and on the other end of the phone, Allison frowned.

"Bri…"

Bri squinted then exhaled. "I haven't told him yet."

"Bri…"

"I've been busy with Raphael all day, practicing for this race. There was no time. But I did tell Raphael about what's going on with me so that should count for something."

Allison pursed her lips. "Yeah, it does. So this time, I'll let you off the hook. But tomorrow—"

"I'm on it. Trust me, I got this."

"Okay," Allison said, satisfied.

"I guess I'll let you get back to your bath, but first, how was today's practice?"

"Would you believe it if I said I'm sore and stimulated at the same time?"

"Yes, I would; you're working with a Valentine."

Bri nodded. "Exactly."

Allison chuckled. "All right, I'll talk to you *mañana.*"

"All right girl, tell Lance I said goodnight."

Seconds later, a dark voice sounded. "Good night, Bri St. James."

Bri shook her head; Lance sounded as if he was on the phone, which meant he and Allison were up under each other, never getting enough.

OVER THE NEXT SEVERAL DAYS, BRI MADE IT HER MISSION TO avoid Allison at all costs. She spent most of her time working out and practicing for the race, wanting to be on top of her game when she and Raphael got together for their final practice.

In between that time, she ran Building Bridges Wedding and Event Planning from her home in an attempt to avoid Philip.

He called her several times, sent emails and left voice-mails pleading with Bri to return his appeals. But the fact of the matter was Bri needed time to get her thoughts together. Even with the revelation that she was indeed using Philip as her Dean, she still couldn't seem to push herself in the direction she needed to go.

When it was time to meet up with Raphael again, Bri was in another full body spandex catsuit, Nike shoes with cleats on the bottom, and fingerless gloves.

With her hair tied to the top of her head, she worked the obstacle course, managing to make it over each hurdle on her third try.

"That's my girl!" Raphael gave her a high five, and Bri tap-danced, then jumped in the air and kicked her feet.

They laughed enthusiastically as Bri stepped into a dance, forward then back in a twist doing the old school Kid 'n Play. Joining her, Raphael eased into her groove, step-dancing forward with a kick of his feet, out, then in again.

"Ayeee!" Bri shouted as their feet connected, and they did the jump swing to change positions. More laughter burst from them, and Raphael grabbed her up and covered her in the shield of his arms.

"Yes! I think we're going to win this thing," Bri said.

"We will, indeed," Raphael confirmed, holding on to Bri

in a strong, passionate embrace.

That night, Bri wasn't nearly as sore as she was the first time they practiced. And she was excited about the event. However, when the time came to put that expertise into action, the butterflies storming Bri's stomach made her antsy, and she couldn't stand still to save her life.

"You're going to be fine. You've mastered this, "Raphael said, aware of her nervousness.

Bri eyed him, trying to swallow his reassurance but unable to stop the fluttering in her belly.

The building was packed as onlookers, a mixture of family and friends along with the racers, piled into the grand gymnasium.

There to root them on were Bri's parents, along with Raphael's parents and two of his brothers, Lance and DeAndre Valentine.

WTZB news station was broadcasting the event. Allison was covering one end while Avery Michelle, the station's owner, covered another. The reporters previously assigned to the event both came down with the flu twenty-four hours apart from each other, but the show must go on.

Standing side by side, Bri and Raphael took in the details of the course. It was circular in shape, with a mile in front of them to start off the race and a mile behind them that would end it at the handoff. It would've been exactly like the practice course if it were not for the twenty-four-foot-long pool that stretched underneath the monkey bars. With one slip, the contestant would be swallowed by the waters below and officially out of the game.

"Do we still not have a clue what the couples race looks

like?" Bri asked, placing her hands on her hips and shifting her weight from one foot to the other.

She was dressed down in her signature one-piece spandex catsuit, hair tied up and Nike shoes.

Bri pulled her eyes from the course to Raphael, who appeared so relaxed in a Reebok black tank top with matching shorts and shoes. His brown skin caught the eye of every camera in the place as they all zoomed in to gain a look at him. The media was in a frenzy as this was another one of Raphael's recent appearances since being at the breakfast café several weeks ago.

"I don't think they'll reveal the couples race until it's time."

Bri nodded.

"Hey." Raphael's hand slipped to rest on her shoulder. "We will win this. You have everything you need to make it. Your determination feeds your energy, and I have no doubt you will prevail."

She smiled. "You're so good to me."

"It's true."

"I believe you."

"Well let's do this then, girl."

She laughed, and he held his other hand out palm up. Her eyes dropped to his fingers then she slapped his hand, then they high-fived and moved into position.

The women were up first, and their partners encouraged them from the sidelines.

"Let's go, Debra, you can do this!" one partner said.

"Annalise! You've got this in the bag!" said another.

Bri got into position then glanced at Raphael whose eyes

zoomed in on hers. He nodded, and Bri turned back to the track in front of her, ready, her pulse thumping, and her gut churning.

With the microphone in hand, the moderator counted down from three. At one, the sprinters took off in a dash, adrenaline increasing and arms swinging as some moved past others in an effort to make it to the course first.

Bri was in the lead, her focus on the tires up ahead and her will to sprint through them high as she pushed her legs forward.

Back in position and waiting for her handoff. Raphael's gaze followed Bri down the track, silently whispering positive encouragement as if she would be able to sense it from afar.

She took to the tires—one foot in, one foot out, scurrying in an easy bounce through all twelve. Raphael threw a fist pump in air, celebrating as she made it to the second obstacle where she climbed a ladder and steadied herself for the monkey bars.

He crouched and watched her, his mouth moving and his gaze heavy. "On three," he murmured. Bri braced her feet, her eyes moving from the bar to the pool below back to the bars. "Three," he whispered.

She took off, swinging with elegance like the wind carried her on a whisper to the center of the bars. Contestants all around her were falling. Some immediately, and some who'd made it past the halfway mark but couldn't keep up the momentum. Water splashed against her as they plummeted, and Bri's heart thundered as she counted and focused only on the platform that was now ten feet ahead.

Another splash of water and someone yelled, "Annalise, noooo!"

With willpower, Bri continued to swing, but her hands were on fire even through the fingerless gloves. When she made it to the final bar, Bri released her hands on an upswing to the platform, and she landed solidly on her feet in a squat.

"Yes!" Raphael cheered, his mouth spreading into a brilliant, beautiful smile. "That's my girl!" he yelled.

Bri could hear his voice, even from the mile she had left to get to him. She smiled and turned her head to Raphael as she held still on her haunches, trying to catch her breath.

"This belongs to you!" Raphael yelled. He nodded, and she nodded back then on an upsweep of adrenaline took to the ropes, climbing up the knots to the top of a net. Out of the twenty-five contestants that began the race, there were only ten of them still in the running for the couples course. Everyone else had been disqualified, and the men on the sideline with Raphael began to disburse as their partners made their way off the trail.

Getting over the net, Bri began her descent and with her, Debra, a fierce competitor, was at her side. The two were the first ones to land on their feet, and they glanced at one another for a split second before grabbing a baton that rested on the ground for their final sprint to the finish line.

Turning completely around, Raphael kept his eye on Bri as she ran the distance, equally lined up with her competition. To Raphael's side, his competitor stretched his arms and legs then cracked his neck, ready for the handoff.

Raphael's gaze trekked back to Bri, then he lifted his

arms and reached over his solid shoulders and pulled the tank top over his head, uncovering his muscular torso.

He tossed it to the side, and every eye that was female along with camera crews adjusted their focus to the brilliance of his dark melanin illumination. Hard angles created chiseled pecs that blended into packed muscles against his abdomen.

He got in position, hand held out, as he coached her to him.

"It's yours!" he yelled. "You were made for this!"

Her speed increased by a hair, and it was good enough to get an inch past Debra. Bri held the baton out, her breathing labored, and jaw locked tight as she pushed for the handoff.

When the baton got within his grasp, Raphael turned sharply, the drive in the force behind his strength propelling him before all the others. He ghosted his competition; and on her knees now, trying to regain her breath, Bri watched him practically float through the tires, sprint up the ladder and take the monkey bars with sheer agility. How she became turned on, she didn't know, but watching Raphael move over the pool effortlessly coaxed a drip from her vagina. *Damn.* He was even better on the main event than he was during practice, which let her know he hadn't given it his all during their drills. She wondered what else he was holding back from her, and if it could be possible that somehow the sex they shared was just the tipping point of what he had to offer.

That ponder made her hornier, and Bri couldn't feel one ounce of shame behind it.

His opponents did the same, some falling into the pool while others made it to the landing. Raphael was halfway up the rope when the first guy started to climb behind him, but it made no difference since Raphael's speed continued to increase as the race went on. Over the net, Raphael descended with ease, and when he headed for the finish line, his hand was up in the air, fisted and pumping in early celebration.

Bri stood to her feet, smiling wide as he neared. She broke into the Kid 'n Play, snapping her fingers in the air as her feet twisted front and back, back and forth. Running up on her, Raphael planted his hands against his waist and joined her dance across the finish line as their feet connected, and they hopped in a turn, completing the dance.

They laughed, and Raphael pulled her in for a solid embrace, both casting a sheen of perspiration in an overlay down their body.

Raphael kissed her forehead. "See, next time you'll believe me when I say we will win."

"Next time!" Bri pulled her head back, her eyes wide with phony horror.

Raphael's smile was so triumphant, that when he laughed, every camera in the vicinity captured his joy.

"What you talkin' 'bout, Willis?" Bri said, imitating Gary Coleman from *Different Strokes*.

Raphael's amusement was at an all-time high as he guffawed and cuddled Bri. He plastered a warm smooch on her forehead.

"Wow! What a round that was," the moderator said

through the mic. "In the lead, Bri St. James for the women, and Raphael Valentine for the men!"

The crowd roared, and Bri's and Raphael's family could be seen celebrating on the sideline.

"In second place, Debra Connell for the women, and Mitch Connell for the men!"

More applause rang out.

"Final round is behind this wall!" the moderator called.

There were five remaining contestants. Bri and Raphael were in first place. The only way to beat them now was if they fell behind in the couple's race, where they would then go into a sudden death challenge.

The makeshift wall moved, and everyone in the building shifted with the display to get a look at the couple's challenge.

The moderator spoke again. "In this challenge, each couple will run a two-mile race except the men must carry the women however they see fit to the first obstacle. Once you've made it to the tires, you each have to run through the tire loops at the same time, or you'll be disqualified.

"If you make it to the overhead rails, the men must carry the women again in a zip-line-like apparatus over the pool to the other side.

"A sack waits at the end of the railing, where each couple will climb inside and hop to the final obstacle." The moderator cleared his throat and paused to heighten anticipation.

"The warped wall as seen on *Ninja Warrior!*" he shouted.

Sharp gasps flew from the crowd of spectators, and Bri's eyes widened as she clutched her imaginary pearls.

"The four-point-two meters up will test each couple's agility, strength, and resolve to get to the top. Once there, pushing the red button will announce the couple's victory, and their charity of choice will receive a two-hundred-thousand-dollar donation."

Cameras flashed, and the crowd went into a frenzy at the revelation of the challenge. Bri's wide eyes went from the moderator to Raphael, and he winked down at her, his confidence seemingly higher, if that was at all possible.

"How are you not freaked out right now?" Bri asked.

"Because…" he kissed her forehead, "…we will win."

He looked back to the course, and she could see his mind moving to create their path. She wondered if he was Clark Kent during the day and had some supernatural power that he wielded at night for the safety of all humanity.

"You believe me, don't you?" He glanced back down at her, and Bri couldn't help but feel boasted by his confidence.

"Hell yeah, I do."

A grin tapered across his mouth, and he pulled her to him and kissed Bri hard on the lips in three quick successions.

It calmed her instantly, and then she knew he most certainly carried some driving prowess that would spear them to the finish line.

"All right couples, get into position!"

They shifted to get in the ready position, with some women climbing on the men's backs while others jumped on their front.

"I'm going to carry you upside down across my shoulders, with your waist holstered against my upper back," Raphael said.

"So, with my head to the base of your spine and my legs sticking out in front of you like tusks?"

"Yes."

Her eyes widened. "Okay…" Raphael dipped, and lifted her suddenly, flipping Bri across the broad bands of muscle and trailing sinew that led into his neck. With cock-strong strength, he lifted her legs and spread her thighs, then wrapped them around the column of his throat. Her thighs rested against the pad of his upper torso as Raphael gripped her limbs and rose to his feet. Caught up on a tailspin of wind, Bri shivered, then crossed her ankles and held on to his waist.

They were the only duo in that position, and when the bell signaled the start of the race, Raphael ran with the pace of a expert, taking the lead as if he'd practiced this run a thousand times.

Behind them, Debra and her partner were gaining, but the two-mile run with Debra's legs around her partner's waist limited the stretch of his limbs.

Raphael and Bri made it to the tires, where he dipped and swung her over his head in a glide down his body. Trying not to be distracted by the sting of that grind, Bri twirled quickly and together, they took on the tires, one foot in, one foot out, never missing a beat.

They were the first to get to the railings, and when Raphael lifted her in his arms, Bri wrapped her legs around his waist and relocked her ankles.

"Hold on to my neck," he murmured, his mouth inches away from her lips.

She held on tightly, placing her head on his shoulders, as Raphael grabbed the handle. With a leap, they sailed over the pool, in a smooth ride heading to the ground a few feet ahead. Splashes could be heard behind them as more of their competition was taken out as they fell into the waters. Like a glove, they fit together, neither of them feeling weighed down by the mission.

"Brace yourself, *amour...*" he breathed into her ear.

"Any tighter and I might put you in a chokehold."

Raphael's simmering laugh ruffled her feathers.

"I seriously doubt it, my love."

They hit the ground running, but when Raphael stopped his momentum, Bri was still stuck to him like jelly.

"Sack race," Raphael said.

She unglued herself from his warm physique, even though she could have stayed there forever. In unison, they stepped into the sack, while Raphael accessed their final obstacle, the wall.

It stood in front of them like the Eiffel Tower, massive and intimidating in structure. There was a visible cliff after the sack race, down a hill which would give them speed to take on the barricade.

"When we make it to the end of this obstacle, we'll get a running start before taking the wall," he said. Bri nodded, her heart suddenly beating wildly in her chest. "Don't worry," he said, "We'll do it together side by side."

Bri nodded again, hanging on to his confidence in an effort to build her bravado. "You with me?"

"I'm with you."

They started their hop, with the crowd going wild and the cameras focused in on them. They were the only couple at the edge of becoming victors, but the wall loomed higher the closer it became.

Jumping into a sack behind them, Debra and Mitch were doing a bit of bickering as they tried to mimic Raphael and Bri.

The moderator took the mic to his mouth. "Looks like there's trouble in paradise," he teased, causing an uproar of laughter to bellow from the audience.

Making it to the end of the race, Raphael and Bri dropped the sack and braced for the wall. She looked at him.

"We will win this." He held his hand out. "I won't let you go."

Bri nodded again, her heart slamming behind her breasts.

"On three."

Bri looked back toward the wall, her eyes taking on the cliff then the up climb of the slope. She cut out all the noise, mentally focused on the task and the sting of Raphael's massive hand.

Bri only heard his voice when Raphael spoke, "Three," and on a sprint, they struck out into a gallop, then headed down the cliff together, side by side, equally matched. While the crowd was going bananas, Bri's speed increased, and as they turned to take the wall, she held her breath and squeezed his hand.

The burn in her thighs attacked her first, but her adrenaline kept Bri moving upward. They were almost to the top, just an inch away from the landing when her momentum began to float, and she knew she would drop if she didn't catch the edge.

Raphael felt it too, and with a quick tug of his arm, he pulled Bri into the solidarity of his chest, dropping her hand then wrapping his arm around her, mid-air, as his other hand gripped the landings edge, yanking them in a toss that catapulted them over the structure to land in a crouch on top of the wall.

With their breathing labored, and Bri's arms wrapped around his torso, Bri's eyes widened as she stared up into his determined face, his nostrils flaring and chest heaving. He stood slowly with her in his embrace, a smile spreading across his magnificent lips.

"Oh my God!" she screamed, looking around frantically. "We—you!" she stuttered.

Raphael nodded over at the red button.

"There's just one thing left to do, *amour*."

Her smile was swift, and together, they lifted their hands and smacked the red button, his hand on top of hers. The victory bell rang, and smoke shot into the air as the crowd lost its mind. Staring into her soulful brown eyes, Raphael covered Bri with the length of his arms, his fingers tingling her spine as he bent to kiss her lips.

And boy, did he. Lost in the suckle of his mouth, Bri's eyes faltered, and her body vibrated against Raphael's as he devoured her lips while every eye, including the ones watching by way of the local news, was trained on them and them alone.

Chapter Thirteen

*T*hey made headlines. Over the next three days, Bri and Raphael's infamous picture, kissing on top of the warped wall with smoke rising in the background, was splashed in every newspaper in the city. It even made national news as word spread that Raphael Valentine was in love with Bri St. James.

Bri was taking the time to digest it all herself, staring down at yet another morning newspaper clipping on her way to her client's church. She mused over the bond she'd grown with Raphael. They were almost inseparable now, finding reasons to be with one another, spending breakfast, lunch, and sometimes dinner since their victory.

Bri knew for sure she would be sore after that contest, but she'd never felt better, almost light on her feet. More than once, Bri wondered if their *friendship* was evolving into something much more.

It felt that way in her heart, but Raphael hadn't opened up to her completely. She would catch him a few times staring off and could sense a struggle in his spirit. And though she wanted him to unburden himself to her, Bri wouldn't push him. When he was ready, if there ever came a time, she would be there to listen.

Bri sat the newspaper aside, then opened the door and climbed out of her Mercedes. The Burberry coat snuggled her inside a thick wool layer that draped down to her knees. Pushing through the double doors, she was met with a new assistant who handed over a cup of coffee.

"Good morning, Amelia."

"Good morning, Ms. St. James."

"Bri. I told you to call me Bri," she said, smiling over at Amelia.

Amelia nodded. "Yes, Ms. St. James."

Bri shook her head, then turned to enter another door leading to the sanctuary.

"Everything is on schedule. The caterer is here, the cleanup crew is here, the photographer is here." Amelia talked on, checking off the list previously made by Bri.

Bri stopped in her tracks. "Wait, the photographer is here?"

"Yes, Ms. St. James."

"Where?"

Amelia pointed across the room to the right of them, and Bri followed her direction. With a camera in hand, Raphael stood like a master in his talent as he snapped early photos of the interior for the bride and groom's collection.

Bri watched him for a long second, excitement building to be in his vicinity again.

"I hope I'm not intruding when I ask this," Amelia said.

Bri blinked over at her. "What is it?"

"Are you two…together?"

Bri sighed. "So you want to know my personal business but won't call me by my first name," she joked. "Sounds like something Allison would do."

"Who's Allison?"

"Never mind. Come on, we need to get started."

"You didn't answer my question," Amelia pointed out.

"When you call me Bri, I'll answer your question."

Amelia smiled. "Okay, Bri, if you prefer."

"No," Bri said. "We're not together." It didn't even sound right rolling off her tongue.

Amelia lifted a brow as they passed through another set of doors headed for the reception hall.

"Is that something you're guessing? Because he's clearly in love with you."

Bri stopped walking and twirled to Amelia. "Did he tell you that?" Her heart thumped as she waited for Amelia's answer.

"Well, um, no, but it's written all over his face in every newspaper I've seen." She paused then added, "It's on yours, too."

Bri stared at Amelia. The girl wasn't lying. Bri was in love with Raphael, and the thought of him reciprocating those emotions churned her gut and stormed her heart with flutters.

"Well..." Bri blinked. "When I know anything further, I guess everyone else will."

She resumed her stroll to the reception with Amelia in tow and Raphael on the brain.

He fit into their excited circle with comfort, though Bri could sense the apprehension in his demeanor. The guests around Raphael didn't seem to notice his unease as if it was an intimate detail that was only meant for her to discern. They shook his hands, excited that *thee* Raphael Valentine was the photographer for their ceremony. While the wedding went off without a hitch, Bri's focus followed Raphael as he snapped pictures of the bride coming down the aisle; again with a veil covering her face and a train trailing from an all-white bejeweled gown. She held her father's arm as he guided her.

Raphael was thorough with his approach, making sure he didn't obstruct their stroll and still getting all the necessary angles.

Her eyes lingered on his rolled-up sleeves, displaying his chocolate forearms sprinkled with hair.

Bri didn't notice when her mouth curved, and she bit her lip, but Amelia did, and before she could point it out, Amelia thought better of it and decided to mind her business.

When Bri's attention was wrapped in getting the cake positioned in the reception hall, Raphael took that moment to search her out. Here and there, he'd seen her milling about, but the ceremony was so large that they had gotten lost in the shuffle, and now more than anything, he wanted to be near her again.

Strolling through double doors, his gaze found her promptly, standing by a bouquet of purple and white dahlias.

He approached Bri, with hands in his pockets and the camera hanging from his neck by its strap.

"*Belle*," his thick voice drummed.

Whipping around, Bri smiled into his eyes. "They are beautiful, aren't they?" she gushed, turning to push her nose back into the flowers.

"I wasn't referring to the dahlias, *amour*."

That brought her eyes back to him, and a blush covered her face.

"Oh…thank you." Her cheeks burned as she beamed.

"I was wondering if you weren't busy afterward, maybe you would indulge me in a bit of conversation in exchange for a stroll down the boulevard."

"Sure." She glanced down at her watch. "We're almost home free. Maybe an hour or two more. The cleanup crew has already begun doing their thing."

"*Parfait.*"

Perfect.

He reached out and caressed her arm. "I will return when you're ready."

Bri nodded and watched as Raphael's strong stride walked off. Stepping to her side, Amelia whispered. "He has other brothers, right?"

Bri glanced at Amelia and laughed, then shook her head and walked away, still tickled at the girl's inquiry.

RAPHAEL HELD THE DOOR OPEN FOR BRI TO WALK AHEAD. Stepping out into the evening air came with a wisp of cool wind.

Bri shuddered and sank further in her jacket as Raphael fell in line with her pace. "This may not have been the best night to take a walk," he said.

"It's all right."

He eyed her with a lift of his brow.

"I mean it's cold, don't get me wrong, but I like the fresh air. Especially after being camped out in that sanctuary all day."

He agreed with a nod. "The ceremony was beautiful," he said. "You're excellent at your work."

"Thanks, I try to be."

"It will be a long-lasting memory that I'm sure they will cherish for a lifetime." Raphael glanced to her. "What about you; ever thought of getting married in an elaborate ceremony like that one?"

Bri inhaled and shrugged, then eyed him from the side with a smirk.

"What, you don't know?"

"I've planned so many of these events that I feel as if I'd have to do something extra, like," she tossed her hands up, "I don't know, get married in the snow on top of the highest building in the world and then skydive out of a helicopter or something."

Raphael's brows rose exponentially, and Bri laughed at the almost horror-stricken look on his face.

"I'm just saying!" Her laughter bubbled over, and she wiped tears from her eyes.

"*La dame est folle,*" he said.

Bri laughed harder as she translated his words. *The lady is crazy.* Her stomach ached as she laughed, and she held on to her belly until it subsided.

"I wanted to ask, how was that event for you? Did you enjoy being back behind the camera? You were really in your element. I could use you full time."

"You think so?"

"Yeah."

Raphael rubbed his chin. "It was a welcoming change for sure. I might be able to help you with that."

Bri's eyes rose. "Are you kidding?"

"Nah. I wouldn't with you, or don't you know that?"

She blushed hard with her lips pursed and her eyes transfixed on his. While they walked shoulder to shoulder, electricity slipped through their fingers as their hands bounced off each other. Raphael paused and turned to her.

"The night is young. What would you like to do?"

Her lashes fluttered as she held his eye. "It doesn't matter as long as I'm with you."

Raphael's gaze warmed, and his heart tugged vigorously. He reached out to touch her chin and took the two steps forward, sealing them heart to heart.

"What would you say if I told you I wanted to be more than friends?" his dark voice drummed.

Bri's pulse accelerated as his head leaned forward, his gaze suddenly taken with her mouth. "I'd say…me, too."

When his lips found hers, a blistering wave of heat completely denounced the wind chill in the air as a crackle of fire covered them in a seal of warmth. Bri's hands scurried up his coat into the collar, slipping aside his neck for a coupling caress. She took as much as he gave, mouths melting as his arms conserved her body close to his.

"Take me to your place," Bri half-murmured, half-purred.

Raphael nibbled Bri's lips, his gaze low and brimming with desire.

"I'll lead the way."

Chapter Fourteen

$\mathcal{W}$hen Raphael chose to purchase the penthouse suite on the fifty-eighth floor of Chicago's Waldorf Astoria, it was for the seclusion, luxury, and scenic views of the city. But as he and Bri wrestled with temptation in the elevator, impatiently waiting for the cab to ascend, Raphael found himself cursing inwardly that he didn't live on the ground level.

Standing with her back against his torso, Bri snuggled in the hardness of his body and the bulge that tapped against her ass. Her pussy was drenched, and the panties she wore were as good as drowned.

The elevator dinged, and the doors opened, but before Bri could step off, Raphael lifted her in an upsweep of his arms, and she squealed as he carried her down the hall into his abode.

They bypassed each room in the suite, going straight for

the bedroom where they made no qualms about stripping each other to the bare necessities. Bri covered his shaft with the only condom she had left, and before she could finish, Raphael's mouth was pressed into her lips. With a spin, Bri's derriere was back against the rigid length of his erection.

"Mmmm," she moaned, rotating her hips in a swinging wine that made his dick so unyielding it speared against her flesh.

"Oooo..."

Her head fell back, landing on the solid shield of his chest as his hands roamed, one to cup her breasts while the other slipped between her thighs. His fingers created a tempo against the sensitive pearl protruding from her plum, and Bri's mouth widened, a choked gasp caught in her throat.

"I didn't ask," he murmured in her ear, "if I could make love to you tonight."

His fingers continued to circle, applying pressure with every rotating spin. "Do you mind, *amour*..."

Bri bit her bottom lip as an electric pulsation beat with each caress from his limb. Hot kisses rain down her neck and shoulders, showering her with a coating of chills that turned her flesh into goosebumps.

Quickly, Bri spun back to him, and Raphael's hands dropped to grip her ass. He lifted her just as Bri's palms landed against his face, framing his jaw as their mouths crashed into one another. Grinding into his inflexible dick, Bri moaned into his mouth, her body torched with feverish desire.

"I wanna be fucked, Raphael," she purred.

Dark eyes smoldered into Bri's, and with two determined steps, Raphael pushed her back into the wall, as his cock dragged against the curve of her pussy, sinking inside her canal and filling her plum to the rim.

"Oooooh!"

Her body arched and tears stung her eyes upon his invasion, creating an instant mist that blurred her vision and discombobulated Bri as her head swayed.

"Ooooh, Raphael!" she squealed.

"Oui, mi amour…." his dark voice strummed.

His heart slammed against his muscular chest, and heat filled his body at each thrust inside her impassioned pussy. Raphael's eyes closed as he inhaled a breath, and when they reopened, his gaze was drowned in desire, nostrils flaring, and jaw locked. His touch was like that of silk, hot and thrilling, sending a flood of scorching chills as his hands lifted her thighs to spread her further.

He sealed the softness of her body against the hard wall of his abdomen, long strokes making her toes curl with each titanium plunge. A sweet fragrance that wafted from Bri heightened Raphael's libido and lured his mouth to her flesh where he sucked one nipple then the other, slurping them both in the heated cover of his mouth.

Her skin blazed as he feasted on her bosom, stretching her areolas in an extended suck that popped off her flesh as his lips scurried back to her mouth.

"Ooooo…" she moaned.

Fire spread from their lips, crackling down their face in a rushing avalanche of tingles. His tongue worked expertly, moving down her jaw back to her insanely sensitized nipples, sprinkling with hot stings under the attack of his brilliant wet muscle. Another moan escaped her, head thrown back as their bodies smacked in reverberation on each pummeling, catastrophic dive.

"Oh my God, Raphael!"

Another hard suck from Raphael's tongue and her breasts conceded to his lashing, softening on his palate and allowing his hungry feast to devour her. A growl trekked from his throat, and his hips worked skillfully as he pulled in and out, drowned in the ocean of her love. Drawing from her nipples, Raphael bit into her neck, then pushed her body solidly against the wall as his hips ground to dig until he could go no further.

"Ooooo, my…bae be!"

He licked up her chin, his mouth covering her face in hot kisses before inhaling her tongue again.

She moaned and purred as he growled and grooved, pressed into one another, making sure to leave no air between them. The wall shook with vibrations as their bodies continued their hard bucks and battle thrashing.

"Baby…" Bri purred and groaned. "I'm gonna come."

He stroked her pussy some more, long, hard thrusts that threaten to crack her spine.

"Fuck!"

They yelled at the same time, then with haste, consumed each other's mouth and held on tight as rocking orgasms broke simultaneously.

Their bodies throbbed, and nerves scattered as Raphael's rigorous strokes pummeled her so recklessly their thighs stung from the sweltering attack.

It was a blistering release that liquefied them together with haggard breaths on a combination of groans, leaving Bri numb and in awe at his expertise. She swooned underneath his intimidating torso, bracketed with euphoric chills that wrapped her in a cocoon as she sank into his chest. And as their bodies hummed with sexual satisfaction, Bri never wanted to be without Raphael again.

FOR THE FEW HOURS THEY SLEPT, BRI RESTED IN THE CUT OF Raphael's arms peacefully, but when there was sudden unrest in her spirit, she awakened to find the bed empty. Her eyes fluttered once, then twice, as her vision adapted to the darkness surrounding her.

The sheets covered Bri up to her shoulders, and while they kept her warm, the layers did nothing to calm her soul. She pulled herself to an elbow, flipping her hair out of her face to trace across the back of her shoulders. The room came into focus, and her eyes swept across dark drapes that were pierced with the glow from the moonlight. The bed she rested in was enormous, and it took her only a second to remember they never actually made it *to* the platform during their rush to connect with one another.

Searching the darkness for him, Bri glanced down to the bottom of the bed where she found Raphael sitting on the floor with his back propped against the bed's base. Bri moved from within the covers, easing down to the edge where his mind worked quietly in the night. There, she rotated to her back, causing her hair to hang off the side.

She turned her mouth to his lobe as her spirit connected with the turbulence within him.

"Let me be your listening ear..."

The room fell quiet again, and she waited to see if he would accept her invitation. Seconds turned into minutes but no one said a thing, and the silence around them continued to stew.

Bri kept her face on Raphael's, needing to read an emotionless expression that was half-hidden by the night and half-washed in moonlight. The first sign of his movements occurred when Raphael blinked, and then he turned to connect with her eyes.

"In three weeks, it will be five years since...the accident." His voice drummed with thick darkness. "As you can imagine, life was increasingly difficult during that time. I suffered from anxiety, depression, among other things, and there was always that inevitable question. Why?" He paused. "My first year of therapy was the roughest. Spilling my guts, speaking about the truth of my emotional state, and admitting the accident was out of my control. It was eye-opening...and worth this healing process I was told would happen, but I had yet to experience." He paused again.

"In the beginning, the nightmares happened frequently, but after the first two years, they became less and less. Now, I experience them whenever her death date approaches." His head fell back, and his gaze moved to the ceiling. "I usually lock myself away, so I don't disturb the natural order of the world with my wretchedness."

Bri's chest tightened as she felt the sadness he endured then and even now as she lay there listening.

His gaze slipped from the ceiling to the floor. When he lifted it again and recaptured her eyes, there was fear in the window of his soul, and it was so strong it almost overpowered her.

"It's happening to you now, isn't it?"

His lids lowered. "It is, except, I no longer see her face." Bri frowned as he held her stare. "I see yours."

Her mouth parted, and a soft gasp escaped her mouth. Raphael's jaw tightened.

"I don't know if I'm any good for you, *amour*…"

Her heart ached for him, and she pulled to her knees then eased off the bed to join him on the floor. She sat in his lap, facing him.

"I can't live through another…what if…I…"

"Shhhh, Raphael," her soft voice whispered as her hands framed his face. "Fear can paralyze a person. It'll make you think a falsehood is true." He stared at her. "I understand that this feels like a premonition to you, and I'm so sorry this is happening." Her mind whirled. "I have a theory."

He kept her eye. "It is possible that you see my face because we've been together. Your past is mixing with your present in a way that changes the systematic advance in your dreams. Have you ever watched a movie, and later that night you have a similar dream, or were a part of the film in some way except you were the star of the show?"

"Yes, I see your point." He exhaled long and thankfully,

as if needing another explanation, for what was happening was dire.

"Being with you, what I've noticed is you're very caring, considerate, loyal, and most of all, a protector. I can imagine how someone who needs to be that protector must feel when it seems as if a circumstance is out of his hands. And you punish yourself for it, even going so far as to withdraw from the world in order to *save* others from yourself.

"When in actuality, we need you. Did you see what you just acquired the other day? The Forget Me Not charity wouldn't have the donation it has without you. Museums around the globe wouldn't hold the risky snapshots of Alaska, or the golden glow of the sky captured at the precise moment in France without you. I would've been stuck without a photographer and likely would've lost my client without you.

"The world needs you. I…need you, Raphael."

His eyes closed, and Bri leaned into him, forehead to forehead, as Raphael's arms wrapped around her waist and held her snugly. In return, her hands slipped from his jaw, and her arms rested on the hills of his shoulders.

"I don't want to be without you," he murmured.

"Then don't push me away. I'm here to stay if you want me to, and I'm willing to face your demons head-on. Together, we will conquer them."

Raphael reopened his eyes then lifted his chin and kissed her lips, soft and steady. "Thank you for being here with me." He kissed her again.

"There's no place I'd rather be." They kissed once more. "Come, let's go to bed," she said.

Raphael eased to his feet, his hard thighs a solid rock beneath her legs as he rose from the floor with Bri in his arms. Together, they spooned through the night, managing to find a lengthy, peaceful rest.

THE NEXT MORNING, THE SMELL OF FRYING BACON PULLED Raphael to a sitting position in bed. Next to him, there was no sign of Bri, so he surmised she was in the kitchen cooking. He tossed his legs over the side and made his way to the bathroom to freshen up.

When Raphael entered the kitchen, Bri stood before the stove with his shirt covering her body and an apron tied around her waist. A spatula was in her hand, and as his gaze traveled down the back of her thighs a storm of heat flooded his veins. Raphael took that moment to enjoy the little dance she did as she flipped the pancakes in the skillet. He imagined her there every morning, with a glow on her face from the love they made and the extra pep in her step; animated.

"Good morning," his dark voice drummed.

Bri twirled around, an instant smile highlighting her face.

"Good morning." She looked him up and down boldly, over broad shoulders and deep chocolate skin. His stroll was the swagger of a man confident in his approach and plastered to his hard thighs was a pair of boxer briefs.

His chest was bare, and a powerful sheet of muscle ran down his torso blending into the cut formation of his

Adonis belt. Bri's body flamed instantly, but a secondary crawl of electric currents crept up her spine as she eyed his footsteps, creating a predatory path to tower over her.

"What's going on in here?"

He leaned forward, wrapping his arms around her waist to pull her in.

"I'm..." A shiver eased down Bri's core. "...cooking breakfast."

He planted his hands against her waist, and his fingers danced to the tie in the back of her apron that rested on the hill of her derriere.

"Hmmm, I should've told you there's a rule I must live by, and I can't have you breaking my rules."

Her brow lifted. "What's the rule?" she asked, hypnotized by the intensity of his gaze.

Raphael untied the knot. And the apron drifted from her waist to rest around his carved cut abdomen.

"I serve you."

He took the spatula and planted a scorching kiss on her lips that melted her bones and incinerated her blood. Heat spilled from their mouths, and her pussy thumped as she was lifted by a strong arm into his warm embrace.

"Loooord have mercy," she breathed as Raphael summoned her tongue, then nibbled her lips like he hadn't tasted her thoroughly the night before.

Her mouth parted, and another moan escaped her lips, desire filling them both and spilling over their flesh. With a quick swat, Raphael smacked her ass with the spatula.

"Eek!" she shrieked then laughed into his lips.

His voice was a gruff undertone when he spoke, *"Amour, amour..."*

"Yeah," she purred, her lips swollen from the hungry feed of his mouth.

Painstakingly turned on, he made a declaration, "I don't mind having you for breakfast, but if you want food—"

"Damn the food."

He crushed his mouth to hers again, dropping the spatula and lifting Bri with the palm of his brawny hands.

"Oooh..."

She panted, moaned, and writhed against his pelvis as her arms fumbled to untie the apron in a hurry to free him of the blockage it caused. Raphael walked her to the island, then sat Bri on the edge as his hands slipped to spread her thighs. His finger danced across her clitoris just as he dipped to place hot kisses against her lips.

Bri's eyes rolled, and her body trembled as sparks shocked her from the sensational caress of his touch. She could never get enough of him, and she wanted desperately to be filled with his love.

Raphael spoke thoughtfully. "We're out of condoms."

Bri leaned into his mouth, sinking her lips into the warm flesh of his. She reached and grabbed his dick, then moaned and traced her tongue around his lips.

A ticking growl fled from Raphael as she freed his erection, dragging his shaft up and down the soft folds of her plum in a hard, undulating press.

"That crossed my mind too," she whispered, coaxing the head of his cock into the entrance of her pussy.

"Aaaaaah..." Her head fell back on a moan when his shaft entered her with a deep, piercing thrust.

"*E ne peux pas en avoir assez...*" *I cannot get enough of you...* he murmured, consumed by her wetness and the heat that swirled around his distended member.

With her arms back around his neck, Bri's mouth held open, and eye to eye, she saw his jaw lock and his gaze explode with fierce desire.

Taking it all the way, Raphael sank into her canal, diving in an exploratory plunge, effortlessly burying himself. His eyes closed for a second, and when they reopened, he palmed her ass, then lifted her bottom from the island's edge and fucked her pussy in long massive strokes that bounced her off his pelvis, hard and steadfast.

"Oooh my God, baby, yes, yes, yes, oh my God..."

The groove of his dick pulled at her walls with each rock into her core, pinging off her G-spot and curling Bri's toes as shots of tingles crowded her clitoris.

"Ooooo ba be!"

She writhed against him, her head turning left to right as if holding on to a lashing that was beating her relentlessly.

Their bodies slapped with a mixture of sexual fluids that slid between their connection and charged their rhythm.

Her body was scorched, and the never-ending round of tingles scattered on an attack to her pussy. She was assaulted by its sting, making her shout and clutch the strength of his arms.

"I'm going to come!"

Raphael withdrew from her sanctuary, then covered her

plum with the range of his mouth. Bri came instantly, soaking his tongue with squirts of her sweet sauce. It quenched a thirst only she could satisfy, filling him to the rim. He sucked her clitoris to the point of numbness then stood and reentered her sex, his hand now slipping to grip her neck.

"Come again," he ordered, laying down a barrage of thrusting pipe so unyielding, it expelled her to another land. Bri screamed and twitched, her face lighting up on a beautiful spectrum that cast a warmth into his soul when she soaked him in wet heat. They rocked in a dance, and Bri's body bucked like a fish out of water as her orgasm electrified the bones that made up her core.

"Vous êtes si belle." *You're so beautiful.* "Sucré et indéniablement enchanteur." *Sweet and undeniably enchanting.*

Raphael held her with a tight grip, not so much that she would choke but firm enough that she couldn't get away while his hips knocked her over and over in an effort to pull her apart and claim her heart.

Against her lips, he continued to speak. "You make me want to immerse myself in your love and stay forever."

He bit her bottom lip, followed by a soft kiss and suck of her tongue.

"*Amour,*" his thick voice drummed, rocking in her core. "Un de plus…" *One more,* he whispered, and with her body wrangled in a thrilling shock, Bri came yet again.

Chapter Fifteen

*B*reakfast had never filled Bri so completely. But being with Raphael gave the most important meal of the day a reason for her to crave it all the more.

After their entanglement of love, Raphael prepared an elaborate brunch, chopping potatoes, garlic, onion, and bell pepper in a skillet and stir-frying it together. On the side, he added low-sodium bacon, scrambled eggs, pancakes, and a bowl of sliced peaches, then topped it off with fresh-squeezed orange juice.

With the plates in hand, he turned to find Bri wiping down the island that they'd just made unruly love on top of.

"I would've taken care of that," he said.

Bri shrugged and blushed. "I know, but you're cooking, so I'm cleaning."

He loved the arch of her eyes.

"You just couldn't help yourself, could you?"

She shook her head with a smile but held her tongue. "Very well."

He added their plates to the surface then blessed their food, and they ate in silence while stealing looks at one another.

Raphael's heart was full, and not for the first time since he'd met her, thoughts of loving Bri forever pranced in his mind. There was something, however, he needed to handle first, and the weight of it wedged against his spirit, its inevitability now facing him.

IN HIS LAND ROVER, RAPHAEL HEADED TOWARD BRI'S studio apartment, navigating the roads smoothly with one hand on the wheel and the other linked with Bri's soft fingers. When he approached the light at Melrose right before the on-ramp to the highway, his fingers tightened around hers, and his jaw locked.

Bri squeezed his hands and turned to look at him as Raphael stared head-on.

"Breathe, Raphael." She kissed the back of his hand. "It's okay."

The light turned green, but Raphael was still frozen in place. A horn behind them blew, then a car pulled around them, its driver sending expletives into the atmosphere. The light turned yellow, then red, and when it became green again, Raphael released a deep breath and slowly entered the freeway.

Bri kissed the back of his hand again and rubbed his

arm, keeping a steady eye on Raphael as they passed the scene of that tragic accident long ago. He released an audible breath then glanced at her, returning the squeeze on her fingers.

At her door, their mouths meshed with Raphael's hands wrapped around Bri in an impression that sealed their warmth.

"Tu me manque déjà," *I miss you already*, he said.

Her lips parted into a high smile.

"Then don't wait too long to come back around."

"Hmmm, I don't plan on it."

"Call me and maybe we could grab some dinner."

"That sounds divine. Where would you like to go?"

"My place this time."

His head dipped, his mouth pressing hotly against her lips.

"It's a deal."

Raphael left before he could change his mind, and now as he pulled to the mailbox of a Dutch colonial home just outside the city, he remembered why this visit was of such importance.

Taking a sweeping eye across the manicured lawn, Raphael's pulse heightened, and the layer of heat that coated his skin was because of sudden anxious anticipation. After Chastity's funeral, Raphael not only secluded himself from the world, but also from Ms. Sinclair. She was an older spitting image of her daughter, and being around her, unfortunately, added to his angst.

Instead of visits, Raphael sent flowers, cards, and wire transfers to an account that only Ms. Sinclair had access to, an account that was previously Chastity's. However, Raphael knew this day would come. It just never occurred to him that it would be to seek her blessing to move on with his life. With his courage intact, Raphael exited his Land Rover and strolled to the door, knocking swiftly three times.

The neighborhood was quiet, and as he stood, footsteps in the distance could be heard approaching. His pulse hitched, but his heartbeat was steady, and when the wooden door swung open, the dark brown aging eyes gave him a preview into what Chastity would've become. He cleared his throat.

"Good morning, I hope I'm not disturbing you."

Ms. Sinclair's soft smile relaxed his spirit. "I never thought I'd see you again. Are you finally ready to let go?"

He studied her with curiosity. "What do you mean?"

Ms. Sinclair tilted her head and sucked her teeth. "Come in, Raphael. I've wondered when you would finally come by."

She opened the screen door wider, and Raphael eased into Chastity's childhood home. Memories hit him like an assailant running off with stolen property, and he paused to get his mind together before venturing deeper into the room.

Ms. Sinclair halted and turned back to him. "Come on in. I don't bite."

Blinking back to the here and now, Raphael followed her into the living room. Sweeping an eye around the space, he noted the last of their family portraits hanging on the wall and upright in frames on a brown traditional oak desk.

"Have a seat there on the sofa if you'd like."

He took a seat but sat on the edge with his arms propped on his thighs and his fingers linked together.

"Would you like some tea or water? That's all I have."

"No, ma'am, but thank you."

"I've gotten all of your cards and those ridiculous deposits you keep sending. Oh, and I've got enough flowers to create a garden." She smirked.

"I wanted to make sure you were taken care of."

Ms. Sinclair nodded and pushed the glasses up her nose.

"That you did. Her father would've been proud of you as a son-in-law, God rest his soul." She watched him for a long second. "Are you ready to move on, Raphael?"

Though he knew the answer, actually saying the words made his tongue stick to the roof of his mouth.

"It's okay. My Chastity's been gone for a long time. God had some important task for her to do. She never told me what it was before she left, but I'll find out when we reunite again, and I'm sure it will be all worth it. As for you...you were meant for something greater as well.

I've watched you struggle in silence over the years, and I've prayed for you, son, as I'm sure you've prayed for yourself. Don't go the rest of your life in pain, guilt, or regret. The Lord's plans are timed and greater than anything we could imagine. Believe that in your heart, Raphael, and set your spirit free from the shame you've tortured yourself with throughout the years."

A glaze filled Raphael's eyes, and he took in a heavy breath. "Do you think Chastity will forgive me?" He dropped his gaze from Ms. Sinclair's, and she unfolded her arms.

"Forgive you for what?"

A long silence stretched throughout the room before Raphael said, "Surviving…"

The tears he held back slipped down his face in a stream that dropped to the carpet. Ms. Sinclair went to him and, after sitting beside him, embraced as much of his muscular body as she could.

"Let it out, baby…" she whispered. "Let her go. You owe no obligation to Chastity anymore, but you do have an obligation to yourself and those around you, who love you and want you to continue living. Chastity would want that, too."

Raphael tightened his eyes as his head bounced in agreement.

"And stop sending me all that ridiculous money. There's no way I could spend it in a lifetime."

He turned to Ms. Sinclair and embraced her back. "Thank you," he said.

"Thank you, too, son." She caressed his back. "Thank you, too."

"Hey, Dee, what's up?"

Surprised that Raphael was standing at his door, DeAndre opened the entrance wider. "Come in. You by yourself?"

"Yeah, who else would I be with?"

"You've been spending a lot of time with Bri St. James," he said, strolling back into his loft with Raphael in tow. "I've got some coffee on. It should be ready at any second." They passed the dining room, heading straight for the kitchen.

"I see you've added some color in here," Raphael said, observing the pop of red in the accessories that sat on his table, in two paintings on the wall, and two leather bar stools that were perched at the counter.

"Yeah, Avery seems to think the place could use a little light."

Raphael's brow rose. "Avery? As in Avery Michele, owner of WTZB?"

"She's the one."

"And she's been here?"

"We stopped by after we left your charity race. She needed to run in and use the bathroom, and we were in the area, so we came here."

Raphael folded his arms and rubbed his chin.

"I thought she was there to report the event?"

"She was, but afterward, I asked her to lunch, and she parted ways with her cameraman."

Raphael's mouth curved into an infectious smile. "All right then," he said.

DeAndre chuckled. "It was a harmless lunch."

"Yeah, but does she know how much danger she's in?"

"Probably not."

The brothers laughed, dark and conspiratorial.

"What about Bri?"

Raphael's guffaw slowed, but his mouth held on to a gorgeous smile. "What about her?"

"Are you two together?"

Raphael removed his jacket and sat it across a stool. He

rubbed his chin again as his thoughts shuffled with the answer to his brother's query.

"I think we're more than that. I just don't know what to make of it. The feeling has a similarity to the tenderness I once knew but magnified by a number I can't comprehend."

DeAndre's eyes sparkled as he looked his brother up and down.

"You're in love with her," he announced.

Raphael held his brother's stare, his heartbeat thumping rigorously.

"To be in love with her, I would have to really know her, right…I mean, to fall into something as beautiful and deserving as love, I would have to sense it when she twirls a strand of hair around her finger. Or when she's nervous or searching for information while online. Or when she kicks her heels on a burst of excitement, actually floating in the seconds she's in the air."

Raphael's smile continued to hold steady as his gaze moved past his brother's face and went into the distance of DeAndre's upscale kitchen. He dropped his hands against his hips, continuing to stare at nothing.

"I'd have to sense it when joy shines through her eyes as she laughs." His voice became a low drum. "Something like that would make me want to indulge in a lifetime of her pleasures, cherishing her in a way that a man would revere his wife." He paused. "I…"

Silence.

"Love her," DeAndre finished. More silence followed. "Is it unsettling in your soul to love someone else, brother?"

Raphael returned DeAndre's stare. "No, it isn't, and that makes me feel guilty."

DeAndre stepped to him and grabbed Raphael's shoulder then pulled his brother in.

"You know that Chastity would want you to be happy, but most importantly she would want your heart restored. If Bri's love does that for you, release the guilt. Embrace your deliverance, brother."

Raphael's throat tightened as a knot formed just as he released a ragged breath.

DeAndre held him firmly, and Raphael returned his stronghold.

The two men pulled away, and Raphael pressed his fingertips to his temples for a squeeze.

"Do you think she loves me?" Raphael asked.

"Do *you* think she loves you?"

Raphael lingered in deep thought, remembering the curve of her smile, and the gleam in her eyes when they were together. He remembered the way she danced him across the finish line and the desire that lingered in the undertone of her eyes when he filled her to the rim.

"She just might," he whispered.

"I don't know," DeAndre said. "You don't sound so certain." He paused. "But you know where to find the facts, right?"

Raphael nodded, lifting his coat.

"I need to get going. There's one more stop to make before I head over to Bri's for dinner."

"All right then. I'm leaving behind you in a minute. I've got a few errands to run myself. Brother," DeAndre said as

Raphael slipped his thick arms and broad shoulders back inside his coat, "let me know if there's anything I can do for you."

"You, too," he said, turning and leaving the building, confident in the next course of action he set off to take.

Chapter Sixteen

The wind was oddly still as Raphael stood before Chastity's gravesite.

A lover of the earth and caregiver of humanity was inscribed across Chastity's tombstone.

With shades covering his eyes, Raphael stood idly by, silently in tune with the peaceful surroundings. A trench coat covered the broad width of his shoulders, and his hands were linked resting against his belt.

His eyes ran across the subtle weeds growing along the headstone, and with a squat, he reached down to remove them, tossing the shrubbery to the side.

"Good afternoon," he said. "You know, all of these years, I've been so stuck on feeling responsible that I didn't realize how selfish I had become.

"You were supposed to be mine to protect, but I failed you, and for the life of me, I never thought I could see it differently. Over the years, however, I've learned quite a few things. One, everything happens for a reason. Nothing is coincidental, and every step we take is in the blueprint given to us from birth by the Creator. You would think that would make me resentful or harbor questions like, why would God allow such a thing to happen?

"Today, while speaking with your mother, I realized what I've always known. God makes no mistakes. Your destiny is bigger than any one thing here on this earthly plane. And I hope with all of my heart, that you and God can forgive me for wallowing in remorse."

He paused in thought before finishing. "Whatever your position is now, I know you're at the top of your class. And I just want you to be aware that I'm letting you go to shine in the light you were meant to from the moment you were conceived."

He lifted his head from the grave, his eyes shuffling around before dropping back to the stone. "I'll make sure your mother is taken care of, and I wish you an eternity of happiness." He reached and touched the engraving, his fingers treading across the words.

"Shine bright, starlight."

Raphael stood to his feet and nodded, his spirit refreshingly redeemed. With one final nod of acceptance, he turned and walked away.

BRI TOOK HER EYE ACROSS THE ENVELOPE THAT READ Internal Revenue Service, then flipped it open and ripped the paper with her thumb. Standing in the hallway of her building, she skimmed quickly over the words, then searched the envelope again to find a check she'd written returned with the letter. A frown created crinkles in her forehead.

"What is this rubbish?" she murmured, her eyes fluttering over *zero balance.* "Am I losing my mind?"

Bri tucked the envelope underneath her arm and went back into her apartment. Lifting her cell phone from the desk, she dialed the number on the letter, then leaned into a hip as she waited for the call to be answered.

It took her fifteen minutes to get a human on the line.

"Internal Revenue Service, this is Chris, how can I assist you today?"

"Chris, I don't want to make this too long, so I'll get straight to the point. I have a letter here in my hand from the IRS that states I have a zero balance on my account. Is there any way you can check this for me?"

"Yes, ma'am, I can. Is there any reason for you to believe that's incorrect?"

Bri scoffed. "Yes, my assets were frozen last month because I supposedly owed, so I'm trying to understand what's going on now." She paused. "Not that I don't mind if I never owed."

Chris chuckled. "I understand. Let me get some information from you and give me a minute to see what I can find out."

"Thank you." Bri rumbled off her name, birthday, and social security number then the line went silent while Chris investigated on his end. Bri propped the phone on her shoulder and leaned her head to balance it in place. She sat down at the desk, sailed fingers over the mouse, and then she typed in a password to do her own investigating.

Sure enough, the funds were cleared.

"Ms. St. James," Chris said, returning to the line.

"Yes."

"Your balance was brought to zero just before the New Year on December twenty-ninth."

"How is that possible when I have the check here in my hand?"

"Yes, ma'am, well you see, the check was sent back because that balance was paid before we received it. Through a third-party online transaction."

Bri's neck rolled back, and her eyes widened.

"Okay…" Her voice faded. "Thank you, Chris."

She dropped her hand and disconnected the line with a thumb. Her mind ticked as her eyes wandered back and forth. Pulling it back to her face, she scrolled through the contacts to Philip's name. If he made the payment, why wouldn't he tell her?

You haven't exactly been answering his calls.

"This payment happened before the masquerade party, and he didn't mention it there either," she murmured.

Her eyes dropped to the papers her attorney drafted, the ones that would give her one hundred percent ownership of Building Bridges Wedding and Event Planning. It wouldn't be easy presenting them to Philip, but after prolonging the decision, Bri realized it needed to be done.

Scooping the papers up, she grabbed her keys, jacket, and handbag, then headed for the exit. At the door, her footfalls paused, and then she turned and trekked toward the sofa. She retrieved her discarded scarf, wrapping it around her neck then returned to the door, making an exit for Daniels Photography.

———————

"For a minute there, I thought you would never talk to me again."

Philip sat his handheld camera down and met Bri as she traipsed through the door of his studio room. Taking an eye from her black boots, dark denim jeans, black jacket, and the scarf tied around her neck, Philip reached to pull Bri in for a hug, but she stopped just short of his grasp.

"I almost did, but unfortunately, we have business to discuss."

"Brittney, listen, I know I messed up—"

"Save it, Philip. I don't want to hear that same rhetoric you spoke the last time we were here."

"If it's any consolation, my business is profiting this year, and last quarter's numbers look good."

"Great because you're gonna need it."

"Let me help you pay the IRS off. It's the least I could do for what I've done."

Bri stared at him in disbelief. That dispelled her wonder if he had been the one to pay the balance. But if not him, then who? Her mind ticked. The only other persons made aware were Allison and Raphael.

She decided she would call Allison after she left.

"Here." Bri handed Philip the envelope.

"What's this, divorce papers?" he teased.

"Something like that," she said dryly.

Philip's brows dipped as he hurriedly opened the envelope then withdrew the papers to read over the content.

"I thought we moved past this?" he said, remembering Bri's initial threat. "I can't believe you drew up papers. Is this your attempt to prove a point because if so, point taken?"

"No, Philip, it is exactly what it looks like. Now listen, I don't want to fight with you on this, but if I have to, I will take you to court."

He stared at her, bewildered, eyes wide and mouth parting in surprise.

His voice was low and profound when he spoke again. "Just like that?" His laugh did not rise in enjoyment. Instead, it was filled with mockery and utter disbelief.

"Help me understand how you can just sue a so-called friend as long as we've known each other?"

"Okay, stop whatever it is that you're doing right now, okay." She shook her head. "You are acting like you didn't steal from the company. You did. So I no longer want to be in business with you. Simple. That doesn't mean we can't stay friends or close acquaintances. Sometimes friends and business don't mix. This is one of those times. Besides, why do you care? As you said, your company is thriving. You've taken what you needed from me, what more do you want? Give me full ownership of Building Bridges, now."

"Newsflash, I don't want to be your friend, Bri. I don't know why you keep insisting that's what we're doing."

Bri gawked, her head snapping back, stunned by his words.

"Are you crazy?" She asked.

"No, but I think you are." He walked in circles in front of her. "I've been playing this 'friends' game with you for what, five years? In that time, you've dated a few guys— okay, I knew it would take time. You weren't the fast type of girl I was used to dating, and I wanted you, so I stayed in my lane, but come on, Bri. For the last three years, it's just been you and me. I thought we were moving toward a real relationship. But here you are talking about friendship again.

No man follows a woman around this long to remain friends. I picked up my whole life in Atlanta and moved here to Chicago with you. You can't really think I wanted to be friends."

Astonishment washed over her face. "You said you were from Chicago, Philip!"

"Yeah, well, I lied, Brittney."

Her mouth dropped. "Why would you lie?"

"Because I needed a reason to come here. I knew you'd never agree to us going into business together if you believed I was from Atlanta. But I wanted to show and prove to you that I treasured being with you."

"Were you ever going to tell me?"

"Maybe."

Shocked into momentary silence, Bri stared at him, uncertain about the entirety of their friendship.

"Is your name Philip Daniels?"

"Don't be ridiculous. Of course, it is."

She shook her head. "Philip, have I ever given you any reason to believe we would be in a relationship?"

"Yes."

Her eyes lurched. "When?" She folded her arms.

"Oh, I don't know, how about all those nights we spent together. You falling asleep on my lap on the couch or when we would go out for dinner and a movie."

"Philip, I'm sorry that you misinterpreted our relationship, and I apologize if you felt led on by me, that was never my intent." She sighed. "If I wanted to be with you, don't you think I would've told you that?"

"I had hoped."

"Was that before or after you decided to take the money and start Daniels Photography? Because I don't call that being a friend, and I damn sure wouldn't date someone who would take from me."

"Why are you such a bitch about it, huh?"

A gasp flew from her lips, and she took a step back, placing a hand on her curvaceous hips. "Excuse me?"

"You heard me right. So you're little miss perfect, I guess."

"Really? I'm the bad guy?" She pointed a finger in her chest. "No. What you won't do is put this off on me. I am sorry that you assumed we would be together. But for the record, you reminded me of my brother who's off fighting a war he didn't start. That's the reason I was comfortable falling asleep in your lap and going for dinner and a movie. Seriously, do you think I would've dated other men in your face?"

"Like I said, I had hope."

Bri couldn't believe her ears. "Sign the papers, Philip, and I'll leave, and you won't have to worry about this bitch any longer."

Never in a million years had Philip spoken to her like that.

"I'm not signing shit." He tossed the papers at her feet.

Bri stepped into a neckroll. "I swear to God, Philip."

"You'll do what?" he said, moving into her personal space. "Sue me?"

Bri's eyes dropped to a squint, and she folded her arms and stood her ground.

"Hell yeah, I'll sue you, and by the time I finish, Daniels Photography will be mine."

Philip lifted a hand and smacked her backward, her feet shuffling as she lost her balance and fell to the ground. A shooting pain splintered up her ass, and she looked up at him, mouth wide and eyes full of surprise.

"What the hell is wrong with you?!"

"I'll tell you what's wrong with me." He bent in front of her so he could look Bri eye to eye. "I'm tired of women like you. You get your feet wet in business, and when the company picks up, you think you can call all the shots. I wasn't trying to steal money from you. I said I would help you pay it back. But now I change my mind, and I'm not signing those fuckin' papers."

Incensed, Bri shuffled with her feet, backpedaling to put some distance between them, but he followed her moves.

She stood up quickly and without another word, turned to leave.

"I'll fight you back in court, Bri! You can't rightfully take what belongs to me!" he yelled at her back.

Pushing through the double doors, Bri jogged to her Mercedes, hitting the alarm and quickly jumping inside. She locked the doors and took quick, deep breaths with a mist clouding her judgment.

Her heart was broken. Philip was not the guy he pretended to be all of these years. As she rushed to put her keys in the ignition, tears spilled down her face, and she wept uncontrollably.

———

THE LAND ROVER PULLED INTO THE PARKING LOT NEXT TO Bri's Mercedes. Behind the wheel, Raphael retrieved the keys from the ignition and reached for the bouquet of dahlias then left for the front door. He punched a code in the pad that rested against the wall. The door buzzed, unlocking, and Raphael strolled through, passed the mail-boxes and down the corridor. When he reached Bri's apartment, Raphael knocked with four heavy thuds against the door.

On the opposite side, Bri was analyzing her slightly swollen jaw, and in an attempt to cover it, swept her mane to one side of her face.

The knock came again, and she closed her eyes and exhaled, then on a twirl scurried to the door to unlock it.

Swinging the entrance open, Bri grinned and stepped to the side, offering Raphael access.

He turned to her with the bouquet. "These are for you."

"Oh, thank you." She lifted her chin on a brief smile. "I've decided to whip us up some soul food instead of ordering out, I hope that's okay with you."

His gaze trailed over her face, darkening at the instant

his eye fell over the plump redness in her cheek. With the stroke of his hand, Raphael tucked Bri's hair behind her ear to gain a better look.

"It's not as bad as it appears, but don't worry about it. I've got everything under control."

His gut locked, and the pulse in his neck staggered rigorously. "You saw Philip, didn't you?"

Bri had never heard Raphael sound so ominous before, his voice lacking the gentleness she was accustomed to.

"It's not as bad as it looks," she repeated.

His gaze darkened even further; black as night almost as if the blue hue had retreated behind the mask. He dropped his hand from her face, and with purpose, Raphael turned and headed out the front door.

"Raphael!" He paused but kept his back to her. "Please don't do anything impulsive. I don't want you in jail. I need you here with me...okay?"

Raphael fisted his fingers, then relaxed his hand as his pulse ticked, blood boiling with intense vitality.

He pivoted on his heels and removed his coat, tossing it over the back of a dining room chair.

"You're right. I'm here with you." He walked to her. "Come here." They closed the distance, and his hands moved up her shoulders as he gazed into her eyes.

"Let me make you a warm bath."

She nodded and linked their fingers together.

"Thank you for staying."

Raphael leaned to kiss her forehead. "I'll always be here when you need me."

Bri leaned into the comfort of his arms, then together they trailed to the bathroom.

It was worth the wait. Six hours, seventeen minutes, and thirty-eight seconds later, Raphael was in his truck headed to Philip's house. It didn't take much to pull his information from online, so while Bri relaxed in a bubble bath, Raphael retrieved the information he needed, then finished the meal she'd created.

They ate, watched *Love Jones*, and spoke briefly about her confrontation with Philip, and when she fell asleep across his chest on the couch, Raphael lifted Bri and carried her off to bed.

He rested with her for a few minutes. Long enough to make sure she was well into a deep sleep, with his mind ticking and thoughts brooding on the anger that built within him. When he couldn't take it any longer, Raphael was on his feet, pulling his shirt overhead then grabbing his keys and jacket as he stepped into his shoes.

There was no fight between himself and Bri. No need to explain to her why what he was doing now had to happen, and even with the possibility of upsetting her later, Raphael would take that chance and hope she would forgive him.

The condo sat on the end of a well-lit street, surrounded by fenced-in houses and a quiet neighborhood. Raphael pulled into Philip's driveway, cutting his lights and engine simultaneously. He exited the vehicle, his gaze spanning the area for any signs of movement.

His neighbors were sleep, and with elongated strides and frank determination, Raphael strolled to the porch and hit the doorbell. Then he turned his back and waited.

―――――――――

Whoever was outside of Philip's house wouldn't let up. Philip was intent on ignoring, but after a split second of irritation, Philip grumbled out of bed and stomped down the hall, feet pounding as he shouted, "How can I help you at two a.m.?"

No answer. The doorbell rang again, and Philip eased into the wooden barrier, slipping an eye through the peephole only to have his sight obstructed.

"Uggggh!"

He unlatched the chain, and when the door opened, the fist connecting with his nose shot a fragmenting pain torching throughout the spread of his face. Philip instantly retreated as a howl escaped his throat, and Raphael stepped into his space and closed the door behind him.

"I think we need to talk, you and I."

He removed his jacket and tossed it over the table in the foyer, taking predacious steps toward Philip as Philip eyed him in horror and backed away.

"You seem to have it in your head that it's okay to hit women, or maybe you're just a street fighter, and you like to throw blows. So, I'm here for you, Philip. Pick on me. Come on. Let's fight."

Raphael's gaze set into an impenetrable mask of fury, and he lifted his arms, getting into a boxing stance.

"I'm calling the police! This is breaking and entering, you're going to jail!"

Raphael punched him again, this time, three quick blows to the face with each fist as if Philip were a punching bag.

Raphael *tsk-tsk*ed. "I haven't broken into your house, Philip," he said. "You opened the door. That would make me a welcoming guest."

Raphael's arm shot out, connecting with Philip's right eye; his howl penetrated the walls, causing a few hounds to bark in the distance.

"You're…" He spat out blood while backpedaling as he dragged his feet to distance himself for Raphael's next attack.

"I'm what?" Raphael put his hand to his ear. "I can't understand you, Philip. You shouldn't talk with your mouth full of blood. It's rude." Two quick steps forward, and Raphael's fist connected with Philip's jaw, causing him to trip, fall, and scramble in retreat.

"You'll go to jail for assaulting me!" Philip shouted, on a final urge to halt Raphael's aggression.

"Oh yeah…that." Raphael shrugged. "It's such a shame there's nobody here to witness this assault you speak of. But here, let me get you the phone so you can call the police. Tell the chief I said hi."

Philip winced in pain, then brought his hand from his face and grimaced at the blood in his palm. When he looked up again, Raphael was in his face, his arm outstretched as he grabbed Philip's throat. Philip's hands rushed to

Raphael's wrists, trying to free himself in a struggle from his heavy grip.

"Listen to me, Philip, because this is the only time I'm going to express this through words." Raphael paused. "Nod if you understand me."

Philip nodded rigorously.

"You will sign the legal documents and give Bri one-hundred percent of her company, and you will never put your hands on her again in your life. If you so much as find yourself in an empty room with her, I'll be there to show you the way to your gravesite. You feel me?"

Philip nodded again as Raphael applied pressure.

"Peees..." Philip fought to speak, but the crush of his esophagus made it hard to breathe. "Peees..."

Raphael leaned closer, turning his ear slightly so he could hear.

"What was that you said, Philip? I still can't hear you. Your English is awful."

"Peees...I ca..." Philip coughed hard, and his face contorted and turned a pale shade of brown.

"Hmmm," Raphael murmured.

Philip's eyes rolled, and Raphael released him in a toss across the living room table.

The slab of wood flipped as Philip's weights bent into it, taking an abandoned Coke and an ashtray with him to the base of the sofa.

Standing from his bent position, Raphael turned his back, then strolled to the foyer where he retrieved his jacket. With a whistle on his tongue, he left, slamming the door.

Chapter Seventeen

He'd watched her throughout the night and heard her speak in her dreams with a soft voice that clutched his heart.

"I love you," she said, her mouth curving into a shy smile.

Raphael's heart knocked thunderously as he wondered who was on the receiving end of her adoration.

"Yeah, say it twice if you mean it," she murmured, laughing again with a soft exhale on her lips.

He bent and kissed her temples, trailing a warm smooth glide down the outer edge of her face. She sank into the heat of his mouth, her eyes fluttering, pulled from her dream.

"It's you..." Bri said.

Again, he wondered if she meant the person on the other in of her affections.

"It is me." He kissed the tip of her nose then brushed his mouth across her lips.

Her mouth scurried into a smile. "How long have you been awake?"

"Hmmm. Just a little while."

Her eyes dimmed. "Did you have a bad dream?"

"No, amour. I haven't had one since our last conversation at the foot of the bed."

"That's good, right?"

"Excellent."

Her hand slipped to his face, and Raphael leaned in for a kiss.

"I'm making you breakfast this morning," he said.

"Me, what about you?"

"Okay…I'm making us breakfast this morning."

"What? No brunch?" she teased.

"Would you like that?"

"I'll take whatever you're willing to give."

A growl trekked from Raphael's throat. "You have to be clear with me when you talk like that, woman."

Bri laughed and giggled as she rolled away from him, and Raphael scooped her up.

"Nah, don't try and run now."

She squealed as he wrapped her in his arms, piercing her with quick jabs of his fingertips to her belly. Squealing, Bri desperately tried to escape his dancing fingers, but it was no use. She was absorbed in a fit of tickles that made her giggle, scream, and submit defeat.

OVER THE NEXT WEEK, BRI WAS BACK INTO THE HUSTLE AND bustle of running Building Bridges. Back-and-forth correspondence with her lawyer brought her to a surreal moment that Bri never thought would be an issue in her life: to sue Philip. She didn't want to dismantle Daniels Photography by putting his business practices in the news, but he was giving her no choice.

Standing in front of her mailbox, Bri sighed and removed the letters addressed to her. One thick manila envelope could barely fit inside as it was folded and stuffed so tight she almost ripped it apart getting it out.

Her eyes sailed across the sender's name. *Daniels Photography.* She frowned slightly, then standing right there in the hallway, ripped the top half with a thumb and pulled the contents from inside.

The very first page was a letter that Bri went into reading immediately.

BRITTNEY,

Inside this package is my signature and release of the thirty percent of Building Bridges Wedding and Event Planning. You now own one-hundred percent of your company.

Her mouth parted on a gasp as she continued reading.

I want to apologize for hitting you. I never should've done it, and I don't have an excuse. I let my anger get the better of me, and for that I'm sorry. I also want you to know that I'm moving back to Atlanta and taking Daniels Photography with me. There's no place for me here in Chicago anymore, and I'm okay with that.

I know how you are, and even though I've put you through unneces-

sary changes, you're still probably right now worried about me some-how. Don't be. I don't deserve you, and you definitely don't deserve me. I'm an ass-hat, and you should be with the one that fills your heart.

Take Care – Philip

BRI SHUFFLED THROUGH THE PAPERS, AND SURE ENOUGH, THE same set of legal documents Philip had thrown at her feet were the ones in her hands with Philip's signature bold in cursive and print.

Bri crushed the documents to her chest, her feet backpedaling as she sank into the wall behind her. It was official. She owned Building Bridges completely. Bri dropped her head and sighed. She would tear up the legal documents to sue him, and while silently, she whispered and wished him well, still Bri felt as if she was losing Dean all over again.

Held up in the hallway, Bri calmed her nerves and forced herself back inside her apartment where she shut the door and quickly retrieved her cell phone.

After dialing a number, she waited impatiently until her mom answered.

"Hey, baby, are we on for our workout this week?"

"Yeah…"

Hearing the melancholy in her daughter's voice, Mrs. St. James asked, "What's wrong?"

Quietly, Bri spoke through the receiver. "Have you or Dad heard anything from Dean, Ma?"

The phone quieted again.

"No, baby, I'm afraid not."

Bri's gut tightened, and she dropped her head and sank to the floor. She folded her legs and stared at the base and fought the tears that tried to build.

"Okay," she said. Silence lingered. "I'm going to call you back."

"Sweetheart, why don't you come over, and we can talk."

Bri nodded. "Maybe some other time. Right now, I'm gonna go to bed."

Mrs. St. James sighed. "Call me as soon as you get up, and I'm coming over there."

Bri nodded again. "Will do."

She disconnected the line and spread out on her floor where she fell asleep with a heavy heart.

HE WAS BACK INTO HIS GROOVE. AFTER RAPHAEL PUT THE last period in his journal, he knew then that the idea entertaining his thoughts would become a reality. Penned on paper was his full experience, from the moment his therapist ushered him to begin chronicling his journey until there was nothing else to add but his inevitable solution. Things he'd suffered, what he'd learned, and how he overcame one of the most challenging parts of his life wrapped beautifully in a story that he wanted to share for the benefit of others.

He put those thoughts into action, deciding to create a self-help book for those who'd experience similar tragedies and could use some guidance getting through.

He titled it *When One Survives*. It was the perfect title,

fitting for his situation, and it tugged his heart as he accepted the revelation.

Being a world-renowned photographer had its perks. When word got out that he was looking to step into the publishing realm, traditional publishers across the globe reached out with interest to sell his story.

However, Raphael had no interest in shelving his memoir for months on end before delivering it to the world. It was an easy decision to self-publish it, and within a matter of a few weeks, Raphael was set to attend his first public book-signing.

Thousands had come out to support him. Fans, new and old, packed into the local Barnes and Nobles with his books clutched to their hearts in an effort to gain his signature.

Behind the scenes, Bri St. James watched with admiration. She adored him to the fullest and was proud and happy that he'd overcome his ordeal. Her heart was full, and they'd spent every possible waking moment together. He'd also confessed that it was indeed him that paid the balance her company owed to the IRS. Somehow, Bri already knew that, but at the same time, she was utterly taken by the generosity of him. It all felt too good to be true at times, and sporadically, she would wake and catch him staring at her.

She'd wondered about his thoughts, but only kissed his lips in an uninhibited tango with his tongue each and every time. Now watching his line stretched out the door, Bri was inwardly delighted in his joy and liberation, thankful in knowing that what he was doing was fulfilling to both him and the ones that sought him out.

"Thank you so much," one older woman expressed.

"After my father passed, I questioned God a lot. More than I ever had before, but I think I understand now. This life is temporary, and we should cherish our loved ones every moment we have with them here."

"And," Raphael added, "it's not the last you've seen of him, you know that, right?"

The woman beamed. "I do, he's probably doing something with instruments or trying to make the band." The woman laughed, and so did Raphael. "He loved his instruments, so I could totally see it happening." Their laughter continued.

"Would you like a picture?" Raphael asked.

"Oh yes, that would make this day even better."

Raphael hadn't taken a moment to sit down. He stood and shook hands, took pictures, and embraced the crowd until the final person was left waiting.

Walking up to him, Bri moved into the shield of his torso where he embraced her and laid a kiss on her forehead.

"You are amazing," Bri said, her chin lifted to meet his ignited gaze.

"Only as amazing as you are, amour." He kissed her forehead again.

"I'd just like to point out, I told you so," she quipped in a jest.

He arched a brow.

"The world needs you. We all do, and I'm so excited to see you here at your best. You deserve it all, babe."

Raphael's gaze softened, and his heart warmed. He

stared at her before his lips moved again. "A few weeks ago, I heard you talking in your sleep."

"Yeah? Oh, brother, what was I saying?"

He chuckled. "You said, I love you."

Heat swept over Bri's skin, and her heartbeat accelerated.

"I've wondered since then who you were talking to. It's none of my business, but—"

"You, Raphael," she said. "I've loved you for a while now."

His heart soared, and his throat clogged as a gleam sparkled across his eye.

"If you mean it, meet me on the rooftop of the Guardian tomorrow morning. Eight a.m., sharp, in your Sunday's best," he said.

Her mouth parted. "Okay…" She eyed Raphael, but instead of questioning, she asked, "Are you busy tonight?"

He chuckled. "I have a thing or two to take care of, but," he kissed her lips, "I hope to see you first thing in the morning. That is if you don't change your mind about loving me."

Bri's smile lit up his life. "I'll be there."

Chapter Eighteen

VALENTINE'S DAY

The wind chill was below freezing, and Chicago was seeing its first hail of snow in weeks. Still, after the long night without Raphael, Bri wanted to make an impression when they joined again. It was the reason she slipped into her favorite dress, besides the fact that he'd told her to wear her Sunday's best. However, this gown was everything other than Holy with the way it slid around her silhouette. It was the one she'd finally gotten in the mail, custom ordered that was meant to be her New Year's Eve masquerade gown. It slipped off her shoulders, a sharp royal blue that meshed against her figure, outlining her shape down to her knees. A small flair at the bottom spread the silky material over her ankles, and she added a sexy touch with royal blue spiked heels.

Now in the elevator of The Guardian, Bri checked her

face in the mirrored door, her eyes trailing over her bejeweled earrings and necklace as the elevator ascended.

Around her arms a black faux fur short coat wrapped around Bri's shoulders, and it was just enough material to cover her limbs and exalt breasts. She looked like an angel—mystic, daring, sexy, and ready for an elegant evening with her mister. So it was no surprise when the doors opened that Raphael's blood ushered an instant trail of warmth to his groin.

A sweep of hustling wind carried between the two and light flakes of snow fell from the sky.

"*Mon Dieu ta belle...*" *My God you're beautiful,* he whispered.

Bri blushed as she drove her eyes up and down his tailored Brioni suit. The way it fit his physique was immaculate and debonair, complementing each rugged curve in his masterful creation.

"*Mon Dieu ton beau,*" she said, responding in the same manner with a gleam in her eyes.

He stepped forward, taking her hands in his, guiding Bri over the step on to the rooftop that was lightly covered in snow. Coming into view, Raphael's family stood to the right, dressed to the nines in custom suits and gowns alike. A smile stretched across Bri's mouth, and her heart fluttered to see their color-coordinated combination. They smiled over at her with a few of his brothers winking and his father Leslie holding a conspiratorial gleam.

"There's something I want you to see."

The dark strum of Raphael's voice brought Bri's attention back to him, but it was quickly disrupted when her peripheral caught wind of a large aircraft to her left.

She blinked then turned for a look, her mouth opening at the size of a helicopter stationed on a helipad a few feet away. Her gaze dropped to find Mr. and Mrs. St. James, Allison, and a few of her distant relatives dressed just as sharply. Bri quickly turned back to Raphael, her heart continuing to skip a beat.

"Babe, what's going on?" she asked, enlarged eyes and heart knocking behind her breasts.

"I have something," Raphael pulled Bri close, "that I want you to see." He twirled her around, pulling Bri into his embrace from behind. A digital billboard sitting high on a neighboring building flickered and its pixels scattered before forming into a moving image.

It was the schematic of his face that made Bri gasp first. Her hands flew to her mouth, her heart rocking in her chest at the heavy gaze that lingered back. Brown skin and mature features replaced the boyish appearance that once was — seeing him rocked Bri's soul, so much so that Raphael felt her tremble as he held her tight.

"Hello, family."

Corporal Dean St. James took his first look at his sister, beautiful in a stunning gown and surprise written on her face. In a live feed, Dean nodded at Raphael, who offered a quick salute himself as the men acknowledged each other.

"How are you..." Bri shook her question. "Where, when?" she stuttered.

"I know you have many questions, Brittney, and while I wish I could talk to you for hours, I don't have that much time. However, I am coming home soon, and if you're not too busy with your wedding planning business—" Bri's surprise morphed into a flying smile, "—I can answer whatever you'd like to know," he paused, "as long as it isn't classified."

The family around them snickered, and Bri's heart overflowed with joy. Tears sprang to her eyes, and Raphael held her tighter. She glanced to her parents who embraced each other with hugs, the smiles on their faces, exuberant, and their hearts full.

"Don't cry," Dean said.

"I'm going to kill you when I see you," she joked.

"See, that's the spirit."

Their family laughed again. "Seriously, I know you've been worried about me, and I'm sorry about that. Know that I am well, and soon we'll be together again."

"When?" Her eyes widened in fascination.

"Maybe the next few weeks."

The depth of joy that rocked Bri's soul was titanic in mass and thrilling all at once.

"You've grown up on me," Dean said, "and fallen in love, I see."

Bri's heart danced, and though it snowed, her body filled with heat. She turned in Raphael's arm, facing him with tear-filled eyes.

"You," she said as droplets ran down her cheeks. She trembled. "You made this possible?"

Raphael was absorbed in Bri's emotion, wanting to put any fears to rest she may have had.

"I love you, Bri St. James," he said. Her heart thundered

and rejoiced as they eyed one another. "One day you told me if you ever got married it would have to be in the snow on top of the highest building in the world." Her eyes lurched. "You even went so far as to say you'd have to skydive out of a helicopter."

"I was figuratively speaking!" Her face lit up as she laughed.

"Yeah." Raphael's fingers danced with Bri's as he gazed into her brown eyes. "I'm not figuratively speaking when I say you are what's been missing from my life. I've cherished every moment with you, and I want to spend the rest of my days making sure nothing ever changes between us."

The droplets of tears now pelted Bri's face. "What...what are you saying?"

Raphael kneeled before her, and Bri's tears streamed even faster as a hand flew to her heart.

"Brittney St. James, if you have any room for me in your heart, I'd love to begin forever with you, today..." He pulled a box from his pocket, flipping the top open with the pad of his thumb.

A sparkling gleam trod across the double French-set one-and-a-half-carat diamond, with two rows of cut stones stacked around one solid rock. She was blinded by its shine and completely caught up in the moment.

"Will you marry me, *amour*?"

She trembled. "Oh my God, Raphael!" She rushed to wipe her tears. "I could never love anyone else like I love you," she said.

His gaze moistened. "And I don't want to live another

minute without you as my wife," he said. Tears spilled down his cheeks.

Bri nodded vigorously. "Yes! You're damn right I'll marry you!"

Raphael's entire face lit up, and on a spin, he lifted Bri in the air as she laughed with enthusiastic animation.

Bringing her back down his body in a groove, Raphael settled Bri on her feet and slipped the ring on her finger. A smile was stuck uplifting her face, and by his side, they strolled to the edge of the roof where a bishop stood ready to join them as husband and wife.

The wind around them shuffled as more snow fell, topping their shoulders with sprinkles of white as the bishop asked them both the inevitable question.

"Do you Bri St. James, take Raphael Valentine as your lawfully wedded husband, to have and to hold, in sickness and in health, as long as you both shall live?"

A shiver moved down Bri's spine. "I do," she said.

A gorgeous smile spread across Raphael's mouth and before the bishop could finish questioning Raphael, Raphael quickly added, "I do too."

Their family laughed.

"Thank you for delivering me," Raphael said holding her gaze, "I know now it's because of you that I'm here. It's always been you."

Her heart soared as Raphael captured her mouth in a torrid kiss that cloaked them in the warmest sensation of desire. With his arms around her waist, Raphael pulled her against the shield of his body so tight it threatened to combine their senses.

"I love you so much," she spoke into his lips.

"And I...love...you, *amour*."

They held each other in an embrace, impenetrable and thoroughly dynamic. Forehead to forehead, Raphael said, "Are you ready to jump out of this helicopter, girl?"

"No!" she shrieked, laughing.

He laughed with her. "All right, all right, how about a tour over the city?" He squeezed her hands and kissed the tips of her fingers. "I'll be your pilot."

On a breathless whisper, Bri responded, "Yes."

Raphael bit his bottom lip. "I love it when you give me permission, *amour*."

He dipped his head again, sucking her tongue as his mouth sank into hers. "You know we're still due for a trip to St. Louis."

Bri's eyes sparkled. "Could we go now?"

On a twirl, Raphael spun her in his arms and led her to the waiting helicopter.

"Let's do it, Mrs. Valentine."

Their family applauded and cheered, and even from the live feed, Dean watched as they settled into the aircraft, the blades lifting them into the air.

"This is by far the best day of my life," Bri said.

"Mais ce ne sera pas la dernière." But it won't be the last.

Bri met Raphael in a leaning kiss, and together, they flew over the city, beginning their new life as husband and wife.

Note from the Author

THANK YOU SO MUCH FOR READING *WITH YOUR PERMISSION*.
I hope you enjoyed Raphael and Bri's story. They pulled so
many emotions from me that this was really a rollercoaster
to write. If you feel the same way and need to talk about this
story, the place to be is my Facebook group. There's a book
discussion two weeks after every release, and I'd love to
have you!

And oh! If you loved *With Your Permission*, leave me a
review and tell me about it! I'd love to hear from you, and
doing so means a lot to me.

XOXO – Stephanie

Connect with Me on Facebook!
Connect with Me on Instagram!

P.S. BEFORE YOU GO, YOU SHOULD KNOW CORPORAL DEAN

St. James has returned from his tour in Iraq, and his story is coming sooner than you think! *wink*

2019 Author Sightings

556 BOOK CHICKS PRESENTS
THE 4TH ANNUAL ATLANTA KICKBACK

SATURDAY, JULY 20TH 2019 12PM -5PM

URBAN FICTION. STREET LIT. SCIENCE FICTION
MYSTERY. SELF HELP. DRAMA. HEALTH.
ANTHOLOGIES. COMICS. TRILOGY. ROMANCE.
HORROR. EROTICA. ACTION. CHRISTIAN FICTION
POETRY. SERIES. BIOGRAPHIES. FANTASY. HISTORICAL

FREE EVENT FOR ALL AGES

COBB GALLERIA CENTRE
ATLANTA

2 GALLERIA PKWY SE
ATLANTA, GA. 30339

BOOK
CHICKS

HOSTED BY:
MICHELLE NECOLE
& DJ MERCY

FILMED BY:
X PRESS NEWS

FEATURING:
AUTHORS & VENDORS

PANEL DISCUSSIONS
GIVEAWAYS & MUSIC
PARKING $5

ATLANTAKICKBACK.COM

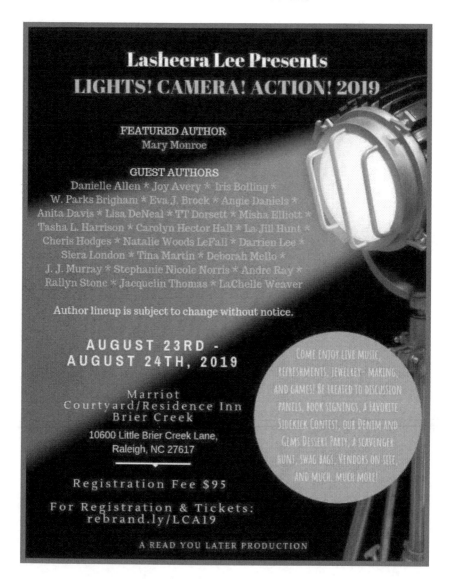

ST LOUIS- OCT: 10TH-12TH.2019

A Reading Warriors Retreat

Featured Authors

Niobia Bryant, Altonya Washington, Lashaunda Hoffman, Angelina Menchan, Crystal Hubbard, Roy Glenn, KoKo Brown, Blue Saffire, Aja, Stephanie Nicole Norris, Anita Davis,Lindsay Evans, Ann Clay, Michelle Hardin,Tina Martin, Jacki Kelly, Rochelle Alers, Carolyn Hector and JL Campbell

Guest Authors

Barbara Joe Williams, Stephanie Morris, W. Parks Brigham

Go to brabonline.net for more information

Other Books by Stephanie Nicole Norris

Contemporary Romance

- Everything I Always Wanted (A Friends to Lovers Romance)
- Safe with Me (Falling for a Rose Book One)
- Enough (Falling for a Rose Book Two)
- Only If You Dare (Falling for a Rose Book Three)
- Fever (Falling for a Rose Book Four)
- A Lifetime with You (Falling for a Rose Book Five)
- She said Yes (Falling for a Rose Holiday Edition Book Six)
- Mine (Falling for a Rose Book Seven)
- The Sweetest Surrender (Falling for a Rose Book Eight)
- Tempted By You (Falling for a Rose Book Nine)
- No Holds Barred (In the Heart of a Valentine Book One)
- A Risqué Engagement (In the Heart of a Valentine Book Two)
- Give Me A Reason (In the Heart of a Valentine Book Three)
- A Game-Changing Christmas (A falling for a

Rose & In the Heart of A Valentine, Holiday Edition)

- If I Could Stay (Lunch Break Series Book One)

Romantic Suspense Thrillers

- Beautiful Assassin
- Beautiful Assassin 2 Revelations
- Mistaken Identity
- Trouble in Paradise
- Vengeful Intentions (Trouble in Paradise 2)
- For Better and Worse (Trouble in Paradise 3)
- Until My Last Breath (Trouble in Paradise 4)

Crime Fiction

- Prowl
- Prowl 2
- Hidden

Fantasy

- Golden (Rapunzel's F'd Up Fairytale)

Non-Fiction

- Against All Odds (Surviving the Neonatal Intensive Care Unit) *Non-Fiction

About the Author

Stephanie Nicole Norris is an author from Chattanooga, Tennessee, with a humble beginning. She was raised with six siblings by her mother Jessica Ward. Always being a lover of reading, during Stephanie's teenage years, her joy was running to the bookmobile to read stories by R. L. Stine.

After becoming a young adult, her love for romance sparked, leaving her captivated by heroes and heroines alike. With a big imagination and a creative heart, Stephanie penned her first novel *Trouble in Paradise* and self-published it in 2012. Her debut novel turned into a four-book series packed with romance, drama, and suspense. As a prolific writer, Stephanie's catalog continues to grow. Her books can be found on her website and Amazon. Stephanie is inspired by the likes of Donna Hill, Eric Jerome Dickey, Jackie Collins, and more. She currently resides in Tennessee with her husband and three-year-old son.

https://stephanienicolenorris.com/

43555743R00133

Made in the USA
Middletown, DE
26 April 2019